GW00863818

GIFT OF GOLD

a story of Ghana

Pauline Thompson

CHRISTIAN FOCUS PUBLICATIONS

ISBN 1 85792 090 2

Published by
Christian Focus Publications
Geanies House, Fearn, Tain, Ross-shire
IV20 1TW, Scotland, Great Britain

Cover design by Donna Macleod
Cover illustration by Heather Ross

Printed and bound in Great Britain by
Cox & Wyman Ltd, Reading, Berks

Contents

Chapter 1
AMMA GOES TO MARKET

'Villagers!' shouted the driver scornfully, as the lorry roared past in a cloud of red dust. The little family leapt to the side of the road, then stood watching as it rattled off into the distance.

'How dare he!' exclaimed Amma's mother, spitting to express contempt as she adjusted the baskets of charcoal on her head. She patted the baby, still snuggled safely on her back and stepped back onto the road.

'A good job you didn't spill the tomatoes, Amma,' she commended. Her daughter wiped the dust and perspiration from her face. The large tray she carried on her head served as a shade from the fierce African sun.

'Where are we going, Amma?' whispered her small brother who was clinging to her skirts. He had realised that they had passed the turning to the small town where their mother usually went to trade. They stepped aside for yet another roaring monster with its jeering occupants, and then Amma waited for her mother to get ahead before she answered.

'I don't know, Kofi.' she whispered. 'Mother has

her best cloth on, and her special gold jewellery. Why would she wear them to go to market?

'Had I known!' exclaimed Mother, as they struggled back from the rough ground onto the firmer surface of the road. She began to laugh. The children looked at her, questioning, for they sensed that there was no happiness in the laughter.

'Look!' She pointed to where the words were painted large and clear on the back of the disappearing lorry. The drivers vied with each other in the use of eye catching slogans. 'Had I known' seemed to have amused Mother. 'If we did know,' she explained in answer to their questioning looks, maybe we would never do anything. I would certainly not have landed myself with three children to support and your father nowhere to be found.' There was bitterness in her voice in spite of the laughter. Little Kofi slipped a hand into his sister's. Both sensed that something was wrong, and the feeling chilled their hearts.

Perhaps their Mother noticed their need of comfort, for she turned to speak to them, the baskets swaying with her movement.

'It isn't much further and then we'll be leaving the lorry road. We can take the short cut along the railway line.' Kofi clutched at his sister's skirt so tightly that she had to release his grip in case he pulled it off. 'What is it, Kofi?' she asked.

'Suppose a train comes. We'll all be killed!'

'Of course we won't,' she reassured him. 'We get out of the way of the lorries, don't we? We would hear the train coming.' But when they reached the crossing she found fear rising in her own heart and wished that she was not too old to cling to her mother's hand. There, on the side of the road, stood a mangled crush of iron that had once been a passenger car. Voices were rising as the ever growing crowd disputed over the rights and wrongs of the case.

Eventually Amma tugged at her mother's skirt. 'Wouldn't we be better to keep to the road?' she pleaded.

'Of course not!' she snapped. 'That driver was foolish. The car stalled on the crossing. He should have pushed it clear before he tried to fix it, but he thought he was in control of the situation. 'No! No! Don't get out,' he told the passengers. What a good job they didn't listen to him. He himself only leapt out just in time, and now not only has he lost his car but those people are angry enough to kill him.'

It wasn't just the sun that brought the sweat pouring from her brow as Amma stepped from sleeper to sleeper. She was seeing a van, tightly packed with village people like herself, crouching like some helpless animal while a snarling, snorting monster leapt upon it.

'Don't be foolish, child,' cautioned her mother, pausing every so often and carefully swinging her load around to look behind. 'The night train has gone. There won't be another. Besides, do you think we wouldn't hear it?'

* * * * *

'You go and walk among the stalls to sell your tomatoes first,' advised Mother, when at last they had reached the market, so full of hustle and bustle. Amma had run into a house to borrow a stool for her, and now her mother was seated, the baby to her breast and her wares spread out around her.

'Oh, let's go and look at those lovely cloths. Oh! How bright they are! And look at these head scarves!' exclaimed Amma, for it was a rare treat to come to the city. She forgot all about her mission, turning aside to delight in a tray of sparkling ear-rings. It was Kofi who had an eye to business.

'Come, Amma! This lady wants to buy.' She dragged herself away, laughing. 'You are a good boy, Kofi. Thank you for asking her. They can't resist you with your big eyes and your dimples.' She went and stood patiently while the woman selected the firmest of her fruit. Her tray was soon empty and the children returned with the money to their mother.

'Here now, you mind the baby. I have to attend to some business. Better not sell the charcoal until I get back. We need to ask the top price.' Mother disappeared into the crowds.

A woman on a nearby stall threw the children a mango each. They sucked its sweetness gratefully, and once Kofi had the juice wiped off his face he lay down on a cloth to sleep.

'How much is your charcoal, Madam?' There was sarcasm in the voice, and Amma guessed that the lad, who stood there in his khaki shorts and brightly coloured shirt did not want to buy.

'It's not for sale. Unless you wait for my mother,' she replied simply.

'Oh, you village girls. Can't even sell some charcoal. All you'll ever be good for is scrubbing pots and feeding babies.'

Amma struggled to keep the tears from her eyes. Of course they were village folk, but when people threw the name at them like this it was hurtful.

'Do you go to secondary school? she asked, as he stood there, expecting some response. She hoped that the politeness of her reply would help to change his manner.

'Of course,' he replied, his nose tilted, as if he had regretted wasting his conversation on one so far beneath him , 'but I shan't be there long,' he added. 'My uncle is getting me a job in the council offices. Then I will know all about the high life.'

Amma was relieved when he had gone. Kofi sat up. 'That one - he is a bad boy,' he informed Amma. 'Why?' asked Amma, surprised. She had not realised that he had been listening. 'I thought you were asleep.'

'I was watching him while you were selling the tomatoes. He was trading with a white man, and afterwards he and his friend were laughing and saying that they had tricked him.'

'It may not have been the same boy.'

'Yes it was. I noticed the funny lump on his thumb and saw it again when he was talking to you. I am glad you didn't make him angry. I think he is bad. He wanted to make trouble for you.'

The sun was high in the sky and the children were huddled anxiously together before mother returned. She brought out a packet of washing powder and began to pour it onto squares of newspaper, while Amma twisted them up into neat packages. 'There now,' she said, 'go and sell those and we'll be able to pay the lorry fare home. And, by the way,' she called after her, 'your Aunt Mary has a stall on the other side of the meat market. She wants to see you.'

Amma enjoyed walking among the stalls again, and it wasn't long before her tray was empty. Soap powder was hard to come by and was quickly snapped up. She skirted the unpleasant smell and the buzzing flies that told her she was close to the meat market, and then spied a girl of her own age. She was sitting beneath the shade of a mango tree, and cutting up large green cooking bananas for frying on her coal pot.

Beside her sat a large comfortable mammy, a book before her on the table. Amma noticed that she would read a little and then close her eyes. She appeared to be talking to herself.

'Agoo,' called Amma softly, as she would when asking entry into a house. 'Amee,' was the response. 'Enter.'

The woman opened her eyes. 'So you are Adwoa's firstborn!' She opened her arms, and though the day was warm, and the embrace even warmer, it was to Amma as a fresh spring of water. She did not know this woman, but felt at once that here was love and compassion. Yet, even as she basked in her love, there came with it a feeling of dread that had followed her all day. Could it be that Aunt Mary felt pity, knowing of some disaster that was about to overcome her?

The servant girl left her cooking and ran and fetched a cup of water for her. Then she placed a portion of the fried banana on a leaf for Amma to eat, as if she were some important guest. Amma ate gratefully, and then took her place beside the girl and helped her in her task. However special her welcome, she was a girl, and her task was to serve.

Aunt Mary sat watching, and then called Amma to her. Wiping her hands the girl came and stood at her side.

'Tell me child, do you know about the book that I am reading?'

'Is it a Bible?' Amma had seen Bibles, but never as close to hand as this. Aunt Mary nodded. 'It is God's book. Come, let me see if you can read.'

Slowly, hesitatingly, Amma began. 'For God so loved the world, that he gave his only son...'

'Do you know the name of God's son?' the woman asked.

Amma was hesitant. 'Is it - Jesus?' she asked. 'Yes,' affirmed Aunt Mary. 'It is the Lord Jesus Christ. Some people will tell you that God has many sons, but this is not true. See, here in the Bible, God's book, it says, God's only son. And we do not have to fear to say his name. Some fear to say the name of their gods, but we do not have to be afraid. We can say his name. His name is Jesus. Remember that Amma - Jesus.'

'Look - here is a small book. It is not a Bible but it has some of the words of the Bible in it. It is for you, Amma. You read it and it will help you and teach you to pray to Jesus.'

Amma was delighted to have something that was her very own. She tucked it into her skirt, then she glanced at the sun.

'My mother will be ready to return home,' she explained, 'I ask permission to leave.'

'The way is open,' they responded. 'Go with God, Amma,' her aunt added, 'and whatever happens, remember that God loves you, and your Aunt Mary will be praying for you.' She did not embrace her again, but once again Amma was conscious of a depth of compassion and of pity welling up and overflowing toward her. She could not help wondering what Aunt Mary knew that she did not. It was as if some sorrow was about to fall upon her.

There was no time to think of this as Mother placed her empty baskets on Amma's tray and then, with the baby asleep on her back and taking the tray on her own head she hurried her little family along to the lorry park.

Chapter 2
THE SLAVE

'Whap! whap-whap! whap! whap-whap!' The sticks rose and fell like pistons. The three girls standing around the wooden pot pounded the starchy vegetables relentlessly. Grandmother meanwhile crouched, dipping her hand into a bowl of water and then, deftly avoiding the descending rods, turning the cassava. Gradually it took on the substance of dough and Amma knew that the meal was almost ready.

She paused to wipe the sweat that was dripping off her chin and running down her neck. Her back ached and her legs felt like lead, for she had been kept on the run through most of the day. No one in the family wanted to accept responsibility for Kofi and herself, and yet each one felt a right to make use of her. It had been, 'Amma, do this!' 'Amma, go there!' 'Amma! Bring me this!' all day long. Amma was strong. As a little girl she had learned to work alongside her mother, but she had never been treated like this.

'Keep going, girl!' Grandmother rebuked her sharply. A few more whaps, and at last the old woman was satisfied. The dishes were collected. There was silence now in the courtyard. As a lump of fufu was placed in each bowl, the bubbling soup was poured over it and handed to the various members of the household.

Amma and Kofi sat apart, watching, waiting. 'We haven't got any,' Kofi began, but Amma nudged him into silence. She was well aware that complaining would do nothing to help their situation. After what seemed like hours of listening to everyone else noisily enjoying their portions, Grandmother scraped out the contents of the pot and called Amma to fetch it.

'There is no meat in it,' the little one complained and once again his sister silenced him.

'Doesn't Grandmother like us any more?' he asked, when they had a few moments together.

'Mother asked her to look after us for a day or two,' Amma explained, 'but now two weeks have gone by. I expect she is afraid that Mother has left us for her to look after.'

'But Mother will come back, won't she?' His lip quivered, and tears were brimming in the child's big eyes.

'Of course she will, Kofi. She promised you a new shirt, didn't she, and she said that if I would look after you, she would bring me a gift of gold. Can you imagine me wearing real gold ear-rings?' She tossed her head in anticipation, her eyes sparkling at the prospect. 'Poor Kofi. And you had to wash yourself this morning. I didn't even have time to help to pour the bucket of water over you. But I will look after you.'

'I managed, Amma. I'm a big boy now.' His sister gave him a hug.

Amma had spoken confidently to her brother, but as the days passed by, her lot grew harder and her heart heavier. Grandmother seemed to be angry with her all the time, though she did her utmost to please her. 'As if I haven't got enough, without two more stomachs to fill,' she would grumble, though she gave them little to eat.

One morning Kofi had been to the stream with the other children for their morning wash. When he came back Amma saw that his face was stained with tears.

'What is it, Kofi?' she asked, drawing him to her. It was a while before she could still his sobs enough for him to speak. 'Osei Yaw says our mother doesn't want us any more, and she isn't coming back ever.'

'Don't listen to him, Kofi. He is only saying it to torment you. Grandmother was telling him that he was a cry baby, and so he wanted to see you crying. He is telling lies.'

She wiped the tears from his face with the palm of her hand, popping a piece of raw carrot into his mouth to comfort him. 'Mother may come tomorrow, or the next day, you'll see. And she won't want to find you crying.' She tried to sound confident, though she was far from feeling it. It was almost a month since Mother had brought them here, and there was still no sign of her.

Nana Kwia, one of the older girls, had compassion in her eyes as she watched this scene, but she waited until the lad had run away to join the other children before she spoke.

'Your mother won't be here this week, or next, Amma,' she told her. 'Didn't you know? That is why Grandmother is so cross. She told her, as I suppose she told you, that she was going up north to trade, and she would be going for only a few days; she would be back within a fortnight - a month at the most.'

'Yes, yes!' Amma joined in. 'she told me a day or two, but I guessed it might be a few weeks. But she is bringing me a special gift. A gift of gold. And she has been gone four weeks now, so she must be coming very soon.'

Nana Kwia silenced her. 'Yes, but when Grandmother went into the city to market last time, she met a lorry driver that she knew and he had seen your mother crossing over the border. She knows that she won't be back soon at all.'

Amma didn't have time to cry. It was 'Amma, run and fetch me water!' 'Amma, come and work with me on the farm!' 'Amma, come and stir the soup!' or 'Amma, come and help to pound the fufu!' She was used to working for her mother, but only one person had been her master then and Madame Adwoa had been careful not to drive her daughter too hard. And of course she had gone to school then. That had been a rest from physical labour, but there seemed no prospect of her going since they had come to this village. The other children on the compound would change into their uniforms and set out on the forest trail each morning but Amma was kept busy at home.

'Did your mother leave money for your school books?' Grandmother asked, if she saw a question in the girl's eyes, 'or do you think I have money to spare?' The girl did not think of attempting to answer.

Amma had little time to look at the book that Aunt Mary had given to her, but every now and then she would take it out of her bundle of possessions and turn it over in her hands before hiding it again. She remembered the warm embrace of Aunt Mary and her promise. 'Whatever happens, know that I am praying for you.' I wonder if she knew that Mother was going away for a long time, she asked herself. It was as if she was very sorry for me, and yet, surely Mother wouldn't have lied. But then she knew that I wouldn't have been willing for her to go without us if I had known.

Suppose Mother never comes back? It was a terrible thought and she pushed it away. 'She promised me a gift of gold. She promised,' Amma said to herself. It was her only consolation. Perhaps it was as well that she was kept busy.

She was sitting with some of the younger women preparing the vegetables one day when Kofi came and squatted beside her. 'Is Wofa Yaw a doctor?' he asked.

The women, overhearing, laughed scornfully. 'Why, Kofi,' Amma scolded, 'You know that he is a weaver. You like to go with the children and sit and watch him weave the kente cloth.' He nodded, but still the puzzled look remained in his large eyes.

'Why did you think he was a doctor, Kofi?' It was Nana Kwia who asked.

'Some boys came and gave him money, and he poured something out of a big bottle into a glass and gave them both a drink. When I asked what it was he said it was medicine - but the boys laughed.

'One of them was that bad boy that I saw in the market.' He spoke quietly, for Amma's hearing.

'Oh, Kofi,' she remonstrated, 'how could you know that? Why should he come out here to this village? It must be another boy who looks like him.'

'But he had that funny lump on his thumb. Don't you remember I told you?' Amma made no reply, and conscious that the others were still laughing at him, he slipped away to join some of the boys who were playing marbles.

It wasn't until Amma was alone with Nana Kwia that she enquired about the kente weavers 'medicine'. 'It is whisky that he sells,' she was told. 'And Kofi is right. There have been some secondary school boys hanging around there. I shouldn't be surprised if one of them isn't Agya Asiaman's son, Kwabena. He is a bad one.'

It was later that same day that Amma was sent across the village to buy some soap from old Maama Boateng. She decided to go via the mango tree where Wofa Yaw was working the loom, weaving the beautiful patterns of the kente cloth. She would have loved to stand and watch him ply his craft. When she saw the two youths however, she was glad enough to hurry past. They were slouched on the bench beside the weaver, obviously having drunk too much of his medicine. She thought she had managed to pass by unnoticed until, on walking further down the road, a stone whistled past her. She turned, startled to see the boys holding their sides, and laughing at her expense.

Amma tried to hurry on, bitterly regretting her decision to come that way, but the boys lurched ahead of her now, barring her way.

'Look! If it isn't our little girl - who had to wait for her mother before she could sell any charcoal. What are you doing here? You aren't from this village? But why do I need to ask? What would any village girl be doing? Pounding fufu, fetching water, sweeping the courtyard, washing pots! That is all you are useful for.'

Amma did not need to look for the misshapen thumb to identify him. It was as if something had brought this boy across her path to torment her. She escaped, wiping away her tears and hurrying on. The words had such power to hurt her because she knew them to be true. She was not only a village girl, but no more than a slave. What hope was there for her? If her mother had not left her, she would at least have gone to school. Even if she couldn't go away to secondary school she might then have been able to learn some trade - perhaps become a seamstress. If Mother had indeed gone across the border she could well remain in this situation, unloved and unwanted. She would be worked to death and have no hope of bettering herself in any way.

'Oh, Aunt Mary!' she whispered to herself, 'You promised to pray for me. Oh, I wish you would pray for me now.'

It was that same afternoon that Amma found herself unexpectedly alone in the courtyard and had leisure to take out the little book. She began to read.

'Why,' she exclaimed, as she turned a page, 'this is the same as I read in Aunt Mary's book - the Bible. Here it is, about God's only son. Oh, if it is true that God loves me so much that he gave his son for me, won't he do something to help me? Wouldn't he even send someone to tell me about him? Jesus, she said his name was. Yes, here it is. Jesus!' She spoke the name out loud, as if hoping that someone would hear and answer.

'Amma! Where are you?' 'Haven't you fetched the water for me to wash?' 'Amma, come and help me to light the fire.' Her peace was shattered and once more the motherless girl was at everyone's beck and call; but as she scurried to and fro she found that she didn't feel so sad. It was as if just a chink of light had peeped into a darkened room to let her know that the night would not last for ever.

Chapter 3
THE PREACHER

'Agoo!' Amma did not recognise the voice outside the gate. Hastily she wiped her eyes, for she had been preparing the onions for the evening meal and tears were streaming down her face. It had been almost a relief to let them flow freely, for her heart was aching. All the other children on the compound had changed into their uniforms and set out to school, but when Amma had dared to suggest joining them, grandmother had been loud in her abuse.

'Did your mother leave money for your uniform? Is she going to send money for your books? Does she think I am a rich woman that she can abandon her children and expect me to provide?'

Amma wished she had not mentioned it. Hastily she picked up a bucket and ran to fetch water to escape from the old woman's harsh words. So now, here she was, left to prepare the meal while the women were away at the market. As for her mother, where was she? Did she ever think of the children she had left behind? Had she no compassion for their suffering?

Amma had not recognised the voice, but, 'Amee!' she responded, 'Come in.' She looked up to see a stranger, neatly dressed in a cotton suit. Kofi, and his playmates crowded around him.

'I saw him,' he volunteered to his sister, 'He was in Wofa Kwame's house. He was praying.'

'Yes,' responded the stranger, overhearing this whispered confidence, 'and Uncle Kwame had to take a stick and chase you boys away, and not only once. Do I lie?' Kofi hung his head.

'It is true,' the man explained to Amma. They were seated on stools now and had exchanged the necessary formal greetings. 'I am a Christian, a preacher, and I have come here to take this village for Jesus Christ.'

'On Saturday some young people are coming to hold a campaign, so for three days I have been here, praying for this village. Now I am going to every house to invite the people to come.'

Amma's face lit up. 'Was it you?' she asked. 'Very early this morning, before it was light, I heard someone singing and shouting. I thought I must have been dreaming.'

'It was me,' he said. 'I was singing praising songs and speaking out God's word. Be sure to tell your mother about the campaign. We will want to borrow some benches.'

'My grandmother,' she corrected. 'Our mother has travelled.' She wiped away the tears that rushed unbidden to her eyes. On an impulse, and maybe to hide her embarrassment she got up and ran to bring her little book and proudly placed it in his hands. 'My

Aunt Mary gave it to me,' she explained.

The preacher had already stood up to take his leave, but now he sat down again. 'Can you read it?' he asked. Amma turned to the page that she had read with her aunt. 'For God so loved the world...' she began.

'The world,' he explained, when she had finished. 'That is you and me, and you and you,' he added, turning to the children. The tears that had been filling her eyes again began to tumble down Amma's cheeks. The preacher was busy looking at the book and pretended not to notice, but at last he closed it and began to speak.

'Sit down, all of you. I have got a lot of visits to make, but I am going to take time to tell you a story.'

'I remember a boy, about your age, Amma, who was very, very unhappy. His parents had died and he was taken to stay with his uncle. The uncle was a witch doctor. He was a bad man. He was angry that he had to look after the boy and would often beat him.

'One day some Christians came to that village. The boy listened. It was so wonderful to hear them tell of someone who loved him; of a God who would send his own son to die for him. But his uncle was afraid that if the people became Christians he would lose his authority. He made the people chase them away. It was his living too you see, for people came and paid money for charms, and for the sacrifices he made to the juju.

'He gave the boy the task of taking the cows to

find pasture. It was the dry season and sometimes he had to go a very long way before he could find any grass at all.'

'One day, when the sun was burning in the sky he at last reached a place where the cows were able to graze. He lay down in the shade of a bush to watch them, but was so tired that he fell asleep. When he woke up the cattle were nowhere to be seen.'

Kofi pulled his stool nearer. He was fascinated. 'The uncle would be very angry,' he began but Amma cautioned him to silence.

'The boy ran here and there, searching. He clambered on to some high ground, but could not find a single one. Despair gripped his stomach and he put his head between his knees. He dared not return to his uncle without the cows.

'It was at that moment that the words of the preacher came to him.'

"When you are in despair; call his name. He will come to you. He will help you." It was as if a voice had spoken to him right there.

'The boy remembered the preacher. He was brave, for the Northerners do not welcome such visitors. He had stood up boldly and told them that God has one son - Jesus. Boldly, he had called the names of the gods that their fathers worshipped, names that they feared to utter, and declared that Jesus was Lord over all.

'The boy had wanted to become a Christian then, as some of the men had done, but he knew that he dare not while he had to live with his uncle. Now in his need he felt the words of the preacher flowing into his mind, like a pool of water in a desert place.'

'He squatted beneath the scant shade of an acacia tree and tried to pray. "Jesus," he whispered, for his mouth was so dry he could hardly speak. "When I am old enough to leave my uncle, I will serve you. Only help me now, I beg you."

'He found strength to stumble on and search some more, but with little hope. Then he tripped over the root of a tree, and as he fell he felt a stabbing pain in his foot.'

Kofi had left his stool now and, leaning against the visitor's knee, gazed into his eyes. 'Was it a snake?' he asked eagerly. The preacher nodded.

'And was the boy you?' questioned Amma. Again he assented. She relaxed a little. At least she knew now that the story must have a happy ending. 'Go on,' she said.

'I tried to suck the venom from my foot, but in a few moments my leg was swollen and I was writhing in agony. Then everything went black.

'I must have been dreaming, for I thought I was back in my uncle's courtyard. I could hear the drums beating, throbbing; bells were ringing, clanging; the calabashes shaking; rattle! thud! shake! rattle! thud! shake!' Amma nodded. She had heard the noise when the priest was calling up the spirits. One child left his stool and began to imitate the grotesque movements of the dance but Amma's stern look sent him back to his seat.

'My uncle was leaping and dancing and twisting,' the visitor continued,'towering over me as I lay, helpless and alone. I was so afraid, but then suddenly the drums were still, the rattles silent, and I realised that someone had placed himself between me and the wrath of the old man. His arms were outstretched, protecting me. Then he turned. I could not see his face because of the brightness, but I heard his voice.'

"I am Jesus," were his words. "You called my name."

'When I awoke the shadows were lengthening, and I knew that I just had time to get home before night fell. I cut a stick to help me and limped along, past the farms and villages, until I could see my uncle's compound in the distance. My cousin was coming along the road to meet me.

'"What about the cows?"' I asked. "They are safe," he told me. "A neighbour found them on his land and my father sent us to bring them home. Now my father has told me to come and look for you; but what has happened to your leg?"

'"A snake,"' I told him.

'"Hey! Mawu - that is what they called me - has been bitten by a snake and he is still alive."'

'Then everyone crowded round to see. The women came to bring me food and made a fuss of me. At first my uncle would not believe, until he saw the mark of the fangs. After that he treated me with some respect, but still I was glad enough to leave his house.'

'He did not beat me, and I knew that it was God's

son, Jesus, who had helped me. He had heard when I called to him and he had saved me. I promised that as soon as I could leave my uncle, I would learn to be a Christian, for I knew that I had no one to help me while I was living in his house. I knew that somehow Jesus would lead me.'

'When I was fourteen, my uncle arranged for me to go and work in the town. The man in whose house I stayed was a Christian. He took me to the church, and helped me to read and understand the Bible. Now I am giving my life to tell other people about him. This is why I have come to your village so that you can all become Christians too.

'But I must go, for I want to visit all the houses.'

'The way is open,' Amma responded. He stood up. 'Be sure to tell your grandmother about the campaign. Indeed, I will try to come back and tell her myself. I want you all to come.'

He placed his hands on the head of Amma and her small brother. 'Lord Jesus,' he prayed, 'help these children to know that you love them, that you are their friend and that you are mighty to save.'

Amma ran to put her book away and returned to her task. The soup was bubbling, the cassava ready to be pounded by the time the women returned. Amma did not attempt to tell of their visitor until their hunger was satisfied. The younger women were excited, for they did not often have such happenings in their remote village, but Grandmother was not encouraging.

'So, you think you can go running off to meetings,

do you?' was all the comment she made. 'We'll see about that.' Amma's heart sank. She felt that there was nothing she wanted so much in all the world as to go to the campaign, next to her mother coming home of course. Oh, if only she could.

Chapter 4
THE CAMPAIGN

For the next few days everyone was talking about the campaign. It was a rare occasion for excitement to come to their village, so far from a main road.

'Now you be a good boy, Kofi, and don't make Grandmother cross,' Amma urged as she tugged her metal comb through his curly mop of hair. 'And I'll work as hard as I can to please her. Then maybe she'll have the meal early so that we can all go.'

'I do try, Amma,' the little lad assured her, 'You know I promised Mother that I would be good. But it is that Osei Yaw. He doesn't like me. It wasn't me who kicked over the pot of water yesterday. He did, and then he told his mother that it was me. And when the baby started crying, it wasn't me who woke her up; he did it. He was kicking a bucket along like a football. But he always tells grandmother that it is me, and she always believes him. Why does he do it, Amma? I haven't done anything bad to him.'

'Hush now, don't cry. Maybe he is jealous. I don't know. He wouldn't do it if Mother were here. Anyway, do your best, Kofi. Try to keep out of his way. And I'll try too.' She sighed, and then added under her breath, 'but Grandmother is terribly hard to please.'

At last the day dawned and the village was buzzing with excitement. 'Amma! Amma! Come and see!' Kofi was so excited. Word had gone out that a lorry had turned off the main road, and all the children had gone whooping up the forest trail to make sure that their visitors had a fitting welcome.

'Oh Amma! Can't you come?' He tugged at his sister's skirt as she bent over the pile of washing, scrubbing and wringing relentlessly. The girl straightened her back for a moment's relief. 'Oh Kofi,' she remonstrated, wiping the sweat that was pouring from her brow. 'How can I?'

The boy didn't speak. He ran to his sister, sympathetically pressing his curly head into her skirts and then squatting to update her on the excitement. It was a great sacrifice to leave the scene of activity even for a moment, but he had to come and share it with Amma, for she was his only comfort, his security since their mother had left them.

'Amma, you should see it. It was like a great monster, rumbling and bumping up the track. We thought it wouldn't get through. There are a lot of young men coming. They have a band! They had to get out and push, and our boys got their bush knives to cut back some of the branches.'

'What about the bridge?' Amma asked, even as she continued with her task. 'It was only made for people to walk over.'

'I know. The driver got out and they talked a long

time and all our boys were shouting, 'Yes, yes! It will take you.' They didn't want them to go away again. So they took as much as they could out of the lorry and all the young men were helping to push and he drove very slowly and carefully and then it was over and we all cheered and the young men jumped in and we all ran behind, and now it is here, near Agya Kofi's house.'

'Oh! Oh! If only I could come and see, just for a moment.'

'Come, Amma! Grandmother won't know. Do come!'

Dare she? If she made the old woman angry it might spoil her hope of going to the campaign. But she felt she could not be left out of all the excitement.

'I'll be back in a moment,' she asserted, and Amma left the basket of wet clothes and ran with her brother.

She gasped with delight as she saw the mechanical beast with 'Jesus is Lord' painted boldly over the cab and there were fresh faced young men in their white shirts standing excitedly deciding where to set up their equipment.

'They have got trumpets and trombones,' she heard someone say, 'and special drums.'

'Look, if we place the generator here, we can fix the lights between these trees.' A young man who seemed to be the leader was speaking, but just then she felt a poke in her ribs. It was Nana Kwia. 'Grandmother is shouting for you,' she whispered. Amma was off like a shot.

Trembling, she picked up her basket of washing and ran back to the compound. When she got there Grandmother was busy shouting at Osei Yaw for going off without having a wash. The girl quietly got on with her task of spreading out the clothes to dry, thankful that her absence had apparently passed unnoticed. She had better not take any more risks. She did so want to go to the meeting that evening.

Amma did manage another glimpse of the goings on when she was sent on an errand to the other side of the village. On the way back she saw the preacher, Osofo Kwesi. He was going around the houses, borrowing benches, and directing the children as they carried them out to the meeting place. He gave Amma a friendly wave.

He remembers me, she thought. Oh! I hope he has prayed that I will be able to come. Oh! I must! I must! Surely Grandmother wouldn't be so mean as to make me stay at home.

The fierceness was fading from the sun as it dipped towards the palm trees to the west of the village. Flock after flock of starlings, like fast moving clouds, wheeled overhead and flashed homeward. There was quiet in the noisy bustling courtyard of Madame Appiah's house as the many mouths were fed. Then, one by one, they disappeared into the night that was already throbbing with excitement.

At last the only sound to be heard in the courtyard was the occasional harsh screech of metal being cleaned, and the stifled sobs of the girl left behind to do the washing up.

Amma had seen the women put on their fine dresses. Some had babies strapped to their backs, while others skilfully twisted their cover cloths into turbans. Amma had made sure that Kofi had on the new shirt that mother had brought him for his last Christmas gift. Even he had gone and left her. Nobody thought about her. Nobody cared. The salt of tears ran into her mouth, causing her to spit.

She could hear the sound of singing now, and the throbbing of the drums above the thrum of the generator, and every now and then the jubilation of a trumpet would wing its way into the courtyard. Oh! If only she could go, but there was such a pile of pots and she dare not leave them. If each one were not spotless there would be trouble. Her tears fell faster. How could she have thought that the preacher would remember to pray for a girl like her. And Aunt Mary. Surely she too had forgotten all about her.

Just then she was conscious of someone crouching beside her. It was Nana Kwia. 'Come on,' she encouraged. 'We'll do it together. It won't take us a minute. You can't miss the meeting. And there is a bucket of water that I have put ready for you to wash.'

Amma would have hugged her, only she was too dirty, and they couldn't waste a moment. With the two working together, the pots were clean and shiny in no time and all piled up and left to drain dry. Oh, the comfort of knowing that someone had thought about her; that somebody cared.

'Don't be long,' the older girl called, as she ran ahead.

Amma never forgot the thrill as at last she joined the crowd that had gathered. It was as though their little village had been transformed into a wonder land. The lights that the visitors had rigged up illuminated the scene. There were the young men playing their brass instruments, while some of the local youth had brought out their drums and calabashes to add to the percussion.

Some of the women who had come with them were dancing, sweeping out their cover cloths as though doing homage to a chief. 'Good King Jesus, Lift up his name,' they sang. Amma thought she had never heard anything so beautiful.

She was vaguely conscious of a group of boys standing at the back of the crowd. They were sniggering and jeering, but she wasn't going to let anything spoil her enjoyment, now that she was here. She had seen Kofi dancing with the other children outside the arena. All her frustration and unhappiness slid away. She cast it from her as she had her dirty working dress a few moments ago. Now as she had slipped into her clean skirt and blouse, she put on her garment of praise, though of course she had no idea that that was what she was doing. She was there among the women, singing and dancing too. 'Great King Jesus! Lift up his name.'

The women were seated on the benches now, the children squatting at their feet. Amma stood with the many others behind. The preacher had prayed. Now he was talking to them.

'We have come to your village to tell you about the Lord Jesus Christ,' he said. 'Listen! some of these people are going to tell you how Jesus has changed their lives.'

A young man came and stood by the microphone. He had on a fine Ghanaian cloth, and Amma thought how handsome he looked.

'Two years ago you wouldn't have seen me in a meeting like this,' he told them. 'You would probably have found me lying in the gutter. I started to drink palm wine when I was still at school. We thought it was clever. When I was earning I began to drink whisky. I couldn't keep a job. I began to steal so that I would have money to drink.'

Amma was conscious of whispered jeers from the youths she had seen, but the people angrily hushed them.

'Then someone brought me to a Gospel meeting like this. I asked the Lord Jesus to save me. Now look at me. I stopped getting drunk and stealing, and now I have a good job and a nice room. I have good clothes. My life isn't always easy, but Jesus helps me. You come to Jesus. He will change your life too.'

The people were on their feet again, singing and clapping and dancing. 'Yes, God is good,' they sang, 'God is good to me.'

A woman came to the platform. 'When I was a child,' she told them, 'I was dedicated to the juju. I had rags and charms around my ankles and wrists. They must never be taken off. Then one day my aunt came. She said, "This child does not belong to the juju. She belongs to Jesus Christ." She cut off the charms. My mother was very afraid. She thought I would die, but when I didn't, she let me go and stay with my aunt so that she could teach me about Jesus Christ."

There were more testimonies, then the preacher spoke from the Bible. He spoke from the same verse that she had read with Aunt Mary. Amma thought it was just for her.

A bench was placed in the middle of the area.

'If you want to ask Jesus to be your Lord and Saviour, come and sit on this bench and we will pray for you,' the pastor called.

'Come, come to Jesus,' sang the choir.

Maame Akwia was the first to come. She sat, her head bowed. Some young men came next. Amma didn't recognise them. Perhaps they had come from the city with the visitors. Three young women, their babies on their backs, ran out, clinging to each other and giggling self consciously.

Amma wanted to go, but she didn't know if she dared to sit in front of all those people.

'Come! Come!' called the preacher.

'Come, come, come,' sang the choir.

Then she heard the lads who had obviously come just to make fun.

'These villagers! They will believe anything!' She recognised the voice and glanced round. No need to identify him by his deformed thumb. She knew it was her tormentor, the one she had first met in the city market.

It was as though the preacher had heard him.

'No matter if people call you villagers; no matter if you have never been to school. God loves you; he sent his son to die for you. All he asks is that you come to him and receive this gift of everlasting life.'

Oh, if only I dare, thought Amma. If only I could, but by now the bench was full.

Chapter 5
KOFI IN TROUBLE

'Yes, God is good,
Yes, God is good,
Yes, God is good,
God is good to me.'

As Amma bowed herself to the task of sweeping the courtyard, her joyful song filled every room of the house.

'Listen to our happy little Christian,' remarked a young mother as she bathed her baby. There was no bitterness in her comment, for they were all enjoying the change in atmosphere that had come with the girl's conversion.

'It is better to see her like this, than stomping to and fro as if she had the weight of the world on her shoulders,' remarked another. 'That preacher has made a difference to one girl in this village, anyway.'

'That's right,' agreed another, ' Now, if you ask her to do something, she dances away as if there is nothing else she would rather do in the world.

'Did you see her, the night of the campaign? I was watching her. She looked as though she was going to come forward, and then someone else came and the bench was full.'

'Yes, yes! I was watching her too. I was wondering what she would do and then, suddenly she ran out and gave the one on the end of the bench a shove, so that they all had to move up and make room for her. Poor Maame Akwia nearly fell off the other end.

'Yes, God is good.' The young woman joined in the song as she swung her baby onto her back, and fastened him securely with her cover cloth. She moved gracefully in time to the music. Others joined in. Even Grandmother stood up and took a few solemn dance steps before going off to take her bath.

'Is Mother coming today, Amma?' asked little Kofi, as he trotted beside his sister to the farm. He realised that something had changed his big sister and made her a happy girl. She stooped to give him a hug.

'I don't know, Kofi. Maybe. She will come one day, so perhaps today. But God loves us. That is why I am happy. If God loves us, then everything will be alright.' Her joy was infectious, and Kofi had soon left her and was running ahead, chasing a butterfly.

They were returning from the farm, their baskets laden with vegetables for the evening meal, and were about to enter the courtyard when they saw that the grandmother had a visitor. They were in time to see her withdraw some money from the folds of her clothing and press it into the old man's hand. Tears started to his sightless eyes, and he squeezed her hand in gratitude. 'Thank you, thank you, God bless you Maama,' he murmured. As he rose to go, the small boy who was with him stood up and taking his hand, led him out of the courtyard.

'That man is blind,' Kofi informed his sister.

'Hush!' she admonished. She waited until she was sure he was out of ear-shot and Grandmother had gone into her room before she continued. 'That is Agya Asiaman. He hasn't always been blind. It is because he is old. But I wonder why he is upset? And why he needed money?'

She addressed her query to Nana Kwia, who had drawn up a stool and was already deftly chopping plantain; but it was Kofi who answered.

'It is because of his son. He is bad, that one. The policeman came to tell his father. Unless he will pay a lot of money, his son will have to go to prison.'

'Kofi!' Amma exclaimed. 'How can you know that?'

'Someone did see a policeman go to the blind man's house this morning,' Nana Kwia confirmed, 'I heard the women talking when I went to the well, and besides, everyone knows that Kwabena has been up to no good for a long time. His father spent all his savings to send him away to secondary school, thinking that this would give him a chance to make good, but he is never in school. You've seen him hanging round the village getting drunk.'

'I know what happened. He and his mates stole a gun and they broke into a rich man's house. They made the man stand against the wall and they took all his clothes, his radio and all his good things. He didn't

even have clothes to wear to go to the police
It was Osei Yaw who had come now to add his contribution.

'How is it you boys know so much?' Amma demanded.

'We were playing marbles by his gate when the policeman came.'

'And so of course, you had to poke your little nose in,' retorted Nana Kwia, giving her brother a flip with the skin she had peeled off the plantain.

'But did you say Kwabena?' Amma was looking puzzled.

'Yes, you know, Amma.' Kofi was bursting to tell her before the older boy, for theirs was an uneasy truce, 'the one in the market.' He slightly raised his thumb, and needed to say no more.

'Oh!' The picture was becoming clearer to her now. 'Poor Agya Asiaman. No wonder he is upset. And now I suppose he is having to go and visit all his friends to beg for money.'

'Yes,' added Nana Kwia, 'and he is not really helping his son, for if he knows his father will bail him out he will only go away and do it again, - or something worse.

* * * * *

'I am going to market in the morning, Amma,' Grandmother surprised her by saying, later that evening. 'If you get ready early you can come with me.'

'Oh, I will, Grandmother, I will.' Amma was

overjoyed. She realised that her guardian's attitude had changed when they found that their dishes had been placed alongside the rest of the family's. For the first time they had received a fair share when the meal was served out; and now to be asked to accompany her to the market - that was a treat.

'You will be good, Kofi, won't you, while I am gone?' she pleaded. 'Don't let that Osei Yaw tease you. Keep out of his way.'

'Can't I come with you, Amma?'

'No, we'd better not ask. Perhaps next time. You'll be alright. It is only one day.'

It was a happy girl who walked behind her grandmother along the forest trail that evening. The old woman had kept her busy, but she had enjoyed moving among the traders. There had been a camaraderie between them that was almost like it had been between her mother and her. Now, their baskets heavy with purchases, they were looking forward to finding the evening meal already prepared for them.

Amma had expected to find the children, Kofi foremost, running up the road to meet them, but it wasn't until they were within sight of the village that she realised something was wrong. She could hear the wailing of a soul in distress, and knew without any doubt that it was her small brother.

Her basket lowered to the ground, Amma ran to gather the little bundle of misery into her arms, but before she could reach him the women from the compound had intervened. They stood between them, their fingers raised in accusation while Kofi cowered, wailing loudly.

It was a while before Amma could piece together what had happened. That Kofi, her affectionate little Kofi, should take a knife and attack the baby; it was unthinkable. But little by little the story became plain. She could see it all. Kofi, comforted in his sister's absence, so happy to have the gift of a newly baked cob of corn. Then Osei Yaw, his tormenter, knowing that there was no big sister to take his part, snatching it from him, dangling it just out of his reach, nibbling at it before his eyes until the child, beside himself with frustration and rage, picked up the bush knife that lay there on the ground and ran at his adversary.

'But they said he had hit the baby?'

It was Nana Kwia who explained. 'Osei Yaw side-stepped of course, and it was the baby who was in the way.'

'Is he'- she hardly dare ask - 'badly hurt?'

'Of course he is badly hurt,' rejoined another, and waggled her finger at Kofi. 'This monster; he could be a murderer.' But at last Nana Kwia got a word in. 'They have taken him to hospital. We are waiting to hear.'

It was a long, dark night, and to make it worse the darkness was seared by a terrible wailing, for all the world like a baby being battered. Amma had heard the awful noise before, and knew it to be nothing worse than the cry of the bush baby, a small, squirrel like creature. How it came to have such an unearthly call she didn't know. The girl lay awake, knowing that her little brother would be lying trembling on his mat, but she did not dare to comfort him.

There was no song from her lips as, the next morning she set about her chores. She felt as if she wanted to keep her two arms covering her head, to protect her from the accusation that was coming from the glances of the women. Kofi had slunk away again to hide himself outside the gate. He knew that there was no welcome for him inside.

Once again they were orphans, outcasts. There was no hope of Grandmother taking their part against the spoilt Osei Yaw.

'And I thought that everything had changed since I become a Christian,' sighed Amma, choking back bitter tears. 'Oh Mother! Mother! If only you hadn't left us! Who is there to help us?'

'What news of the baby? How is he?' One and another from the different houses came to enquire, for news quickly spread in a village.

'No thanks to that boy if he isn't dead,' was the grandmother's helpful comment. 'They aren't back from the hospital yet. We are waiting to hear.'

'Don't worry Amma,' Nana Kwia tried to comfort her. 'I am sure it wasn't serious,' but it was past midday, and still there was no news from the city. The girl was beside herself with anxiety, while Kofi, his tears run dry except for an occasional sob, sat huddled against the wall, a pathetic little outcast. At last they heard a shout.

'There is a car, down by the bridge.' The children ran ahead while Amma stood with the women by the gate.

'O Lord Jesus,' she murmured, though she felt too afraid even to pray. But the words of the preacher, when he had related his story came to her now,

'When there is no one to help you, call my name.'

'Jesus!' again she whispered, 'Jesus!'

Chapter 6
A BIBLE FOR AMMA

'Sunday School! Sunday School! The preacher wants all the children to come to Sunday School.' A child ran round the village, ringing a bell and pausing by each compound to repeat the message. It wasn't Sunday, but the people understood that the pastor came when he was able. When he did, those who had a desire would take their lamps and gather around him in one courtyard or another, for as yet they had no church. But a special service for the children! This was something new.

'Come Kofi! Get washed and I will get a shirt ready for you,' pleaded Amma. She knew that there was no use in asking if she could go, for the meal was not yet prepared, but she thought that this might help to bring a light back into her brother's eyes. It was no use, for the child sat slumped against the wall, cloaked in his misery, sullenly shaking his head.

She had thought that when the baby was brought back safe and well from the hospital their troubles would have been over. It was evident to all then that it had only been a flesh wound. Why, he wasn't even wearing a bandage now. The whole incident had been blown up out of all proportion just because it was one of the unwanted children who had been involved. Soon the whole affair would be forgotten, except that Osei Yaw would not let the little boy forget. He seemed determined to continue his persecution.

'Kofi, please go,' pleaded Amma, pulling her brother to his feet, but his only response was to turn and press his face to the wall. Just then the grandmother came in through the gate.

'Here, you children. Didn't you hear the message? Go quickly and get washed. You too, Kofi. We've had enough of this sulking around. And you, Osei Yaw.'

The older boy already had his finger raised to mock Kofi, but now he saw the stick in his grandmother's hand and ran with the other children to the stream.

It wasn't long before Amma could hear the sound of singing and clapping coming from beneath the mango tree. She managed to come within earshot once or twice as she hurried about her tasks but she had not dared to ask if she could go. She was sitting on a stool, stirring the soup and wondering how Kofi was getting on, and whether, even in Sunday School he was safe from his tormentor, when she felt herself being pushed from her seat.

'Here! Give it to me,' commanded Maame Appiah, taking the spoon from her. 'Run along to Sunday School if you want to.'

It must be nearly over by now, thought the girl.

No time to wash or she would miss it altogether. 'O, thank you, Grandmother,' Amma gasped in her surprise, and ran to join the group beneath the mango tree.

If Amma had been surprised by her guardian's unexpected kindness, she was even more surprised by the sight that met her eyes, there, beneath the leafy shade.

Benches had been placed to form a square, but now the children had left their seats and were singing and dancing within the open space.

'I have a friend, his name is Jesus,

I hold his hand, take him as friend.'

They danced around, and when they came to the word 'friend,' they would embrace the one nearest to them. Amma saw the pastor was among them, joyfully gathering two or three of them at a time into his arms, but her eyes were searching for her small brother. Where was he? Was he still rejected, unwanted, even in this atmosphere of joy?

'Once more,' Pastor Kwesi called. They were all getting breathless. As they came to the words, 'Take him as friend,' Kofi and Osei Yaw found themselves standing face to face. They stood for a moment, hesitant, and then - it happened. Osei Yaw put out his arms, and the little boy responded. Their arms were around each other. They began to laugh. Amma was laughing. Then everyone was laughing. They were laughing because they were happy. Jesus was their friend and they loved him.

'What happened, Kofi?' Amma asked, the next time they were alone.

'I don't know, Amma. I had been so unhappy. I thought everyone hated me. But the Pastor was telling us that God loves us and forgives us because, - because -'

'That's right, Kofi, because Jesus died in our place.'

'Yes, and that we must be happy because Jesus loves us, even if other people hate us, and then -'

'And then you knew that Jesus loved you?' Amma could see that she had to help him out in telling his story.

'And suddenly I didn't want to kill Osei Yaw any more.'

'Oh, Kofi!' She hugged the little boy to her. 'Go on,' she commanded. 'Then what about the song?'

'I don't know. We were all so happy. And I just felt I loved Jesus and wanted to give him a hug and then Osei Yaw was there, and we just hugged each other.'

'O, Kofi! Kofi!' She felt choked with happiness. 'If Jesus can make Osei Yaw friends with you, he can do anything in the whole world.'

'Even bring Mother back?'

'Amma!' Her brother's question was still ringing in her ears, as she ran in response to her grandmother's call. He can, she thought, I know he can. Once again there was a lightness in her step, and it wasn't long before she had the women joining in her song.

'I have a friend, His name is Jesus.' She got to the words, 'Take him as friend,' just as she was passing Kofi, and she side stepped to give him a little hug. It was then that she replied to his question.

'He can bring Mother back, Kofi. Jesus can do anything, so we are going to ask him.

Every night and every morning we will pray and ask him.'

* * * * *

'What are you doing, Amma?' asked Kofi, a few days later. The sun was high in the heavens and the little ones Amma had been left to mind were asleep.

'I'm making baskets.'

'For the grandmother?'

'No, for me, - but she said I could,' she hastened to add. 'I'm going to sell them because I want money to buy a Bible. Pastor Kwesi is going to Accra, and he said that if anyone would give him the money, he would bring one back for us. He has heard that the man from the Bible Society has some. But we have to have the money by Saturday, for he is coming then to get it.'

'Oh! A Bible of your own! Then you will read to me?' Kofi was enthusiastic. 'Can I help you, Amma?'

'Oh Kofi, you are a good boy. Yes, you can. Could you go and gather some more of these rushes for me? That would save me a lot of time. Do you know where to go?'

'I know, Amma.' It was Kwaku, another of the children. 'I'll go with him, and we'll ask at some of the houses if anyone will buy one of your baskets.'

Early morning and late at night, the little basket maker sat weaving the rushes in and out.

'Why are you crying, Amma?' asked Kofi. It was Friday afternoon, and Amma had paused to count out her money. 'I need seven more cedis. I've worked so hard. And Grandmother has been kind and took some to the market to sell for me. But I'm not going to have enough, for the pastor .comes tomorrow. And oh, I did so want a Bible. I've learnt my little book off by heart and the preacher tells us so many stories that I don't know and I want to read it for myself. And if I don't get one now they may not have any more at the Bible society for a long time.'

'Couldn't we pray?' Kofi suggested.

'O Kofi!' Amma was impatient. 'I have been praying all the time. I really thought Jesus was helping me when last night Grandmother made the other girls help with the meal so I could finish my basket. But now..' She paused and the smile that broke over her face through her tears was like a rainbow in a stormy sky. 'Anyway, it isn't Saturday yet, so I'll just keep on working, and you keep on praying.'

It was later that afternoon that the news came that Grandfather was on his way.

'Oh Amma! Aren't you coming?' cried Kofi, trying to drag his sister to her feet, for all the other children of the household had gone whooping along the road to meet him. He was a long distance lorry driver and his rare visits usually meant gifts for them all. But Amma continued to ply herself to her basket work.

'Best stay here, Kofi,' she advised. 'He may not be very pleased when he knows that Mother has left us here. He'll say we are just two more mouths to feed, like grandmother did. Anyway, I must get on and finish this basket.'

Kofi was disappointed, but he loyally stayed with his sister for a while before going to view Grandfather from afar. The heat was going out of the sun, and she was expecting to be summoned at any moment to help pound the fufu when she became conscious of a shadow. She looked up into the kind eyes of a stranger. It must be the grandfather. She jumped to her feet and bobbed, keeping her eyes respectfully downcast. But she felt her chin tilted, and found herself looking into kind, twinkly eyes amid frizzy greying eyebrows.

'So this is Adwoa's firstborn,' he commented, pinching her cheek.

'And this is my brother, Kofi, sir,' pulling forward her little shadow.

'So, - your mother thought it more important to go trading than to care for her family, did she?' he asked. 'She has the baby, Akusia, with her,' spoke up Amma, swift to come to her mother's defence. 'And she promised to bring me back a gift of gold if I would take care of Kofi.'

'Gold, eh?' Grandfather mused. 'There are some things that are more precious to a child, I should think.

'But what are you doing? Doesn't the grandmother give you enough work to keep you out of mischief?' He picked up the basket Amma was working on and examined it.

'Amma wants to buy a Bible,' Kofi explained. 'The pastor is going to Accra, but he has got to have the money by tomorrow.'

'And you have enough?'

'No, sir.' Sadly she shook her head. 'Even if I sell this basket, I'll still need seven more cedis.'

'And I've been praying and praying,' asserted Kofi.

The grandfather began to feel beneath his cloth as though to bring out his purse. Then, 'No,' he declared. 'I'll tell you what. I'll make a bargain with you. I am going out soon to set my traps. Now then, young man, if you are so good at praying, you pray that all four traps will be full. If they are, I'll give Amma the rest of the money she needs for a Bible.'

'Oh! That's wonderful,' exclaimed Kofi when Grandfather had gone on his way, but Amma was not so sure. Four traps. It wasn't possible that all of them should be full.

'Pray, Amma. You said that Jesus could do anything.' Amma did pray, but even so it was with apprehension that, very early the next morning, she heard the grandfather stirring and knew that he was going to inspect his traps. Was it possible that all four of them should have caught something? And if they weren't all full, what hope was there of her getting her

Bible? Quietly she wakened Kofi, and the children crept out after him.

Chapter 7
AMMA GOES TO SCHOOL

'Amma! Amma! Did Grandfather give you the money?' Kofi danced excitedly around his sister as she did battle with the dirty washing beside the stream. Briefly she shook her head. She wrung out a skirt and tossed it into the basket before she spoke.

'He said all four traps must be full. Are you sure it was all four Kofi?'

'Of course I am, Amma.' The child was indignant. 'I've told you. When he found an antelope in the first one he was so happy, he wasn't going to bother to look for the others. But I made him, Amma. I wanted him to keep his promise.'

'You are good Kofi. What would I do without you?' and she paused in her labour to give him a little hug. 'I was going to come, but Grandmother called me to fetch water. Go on - tell me again.'

'There was a squirrel in the next one. "That will make a nice stew for us tonight," he said. And then there was a grass cutter in the next one. "Well, that's more than enough for one day," he said, and made out he was going back home, but I knew that he was teasing. And then he said he couldn't remember where the next trap was and we were all shouting at him and jumping up and down, because all the children had come by now, and they knew about his promise. So then he went and found the next trap, but when he saw there was another antelope, bigger even than the first one, he went all quiet and he crossed himself and he was mumbling something quietly. Then he put his hand on my head and he said, "I can see that I will have to learn to pray." Oh, surely, surely he will give you the money Amma. Shall I ask him?'

'No, don't do that. He might be angry. He promised, didn't he? He can't forget, for everyone is talking about his traps being full.'

'Amma! The preacher is coming!'

Amma continued to rub the soap into a lather, as if she had not heard.

'Amma,' her brother pleaded, 'Go and get your money.'

'How can I?' she mumbled, keeping her head bowed. 'I haven't got enough.'

'Hey! Come on now, Amma!' It was Nana Kwia, who had been sent to fetch her. 'I thought you were supposed to be a Christian. Doesn't God answer prayer anymore? What about a bit of faith?' and she took the wet cloth from her hand before giving her a push in the direction of the house.

Obediently she ran and gathered up the bundle of money for which she had worked so hard and went, diffidently joining the little company that had gathered around the pastor, for she didn't know what she should do.

'That is one for you, Maame Yaa, and for you, Uncle Kofi.' He was writing the names in his book as he stored the money safely away.

'What about Amma? Have you got her name down?' Everyone looked round in surprise. It was the grandfather. Amma bounded forward, her fears melted away like the morning mist. 'Here,' she asserted, counting into Pastor Kwesi's hand her hard won coins, and then Grandfather opened his purse and counted out the remainder of the money.

'You have taught these children well,' he commended the young minister. 'I can see that I will have to come and listen to your teaching, and learn to pray like them.' And he repeated to him the story of the bargain he had made with them.

* * * * *

'Is it today, Amma?' 'Will he bring your Bible today?' It wasn't just Kofi who was asking. All the children were excited about Amma getting her Bible. 'Why, don't be so impatient,' she would tell them, but in her heart she was as anxious as they were and she waited expectantly for the call to say that the pastor was on his way.

'Perhaps he couldn't get them. Maybe they had sold out before he got there.' There were plenty to dampen her hopes. But Kofi was her constant encouragement. 'Didn't God send Grandfather just when we needed him? And didn't God fill his traps when we prayed?' She knew it was true. 'When I get my Bible, I will be the happiest girl in the world,' she thought, and once again she was singing her way through her tasks. 'Yes, God is good, God is good to me,' could be heard ringing throughout the village.

But when at last she had her precious Bible it did not bring her the joy that she had thought.

'Amma! Where are you?' Grandmother would shout. 'Have you got your nose in that book again?' The old woman had been willing to give her a little leisure when she had been working on her baskets, but she considered reading to be only idleness. 'If I see you lazing about with that book any more I shall take it from you,' she declared, and Amma knew that she meant it.

There was no longer any song from Amma as she was kept on the run with her various chores. Even the people in the village noticed it. 'Why did God help me to get a Bible if I don't ever have a chance to read it,' the girl was complaining to herself.

'Maame Akwia wants you,' whispered a girl to Amma one morning, as she stood patiently with her bucket, waiting for her turn at the well. 'Here, I'll get the water for you,' and she stood in her place while Amma ran off.

Maame Akwia was sitting patiently grinding some leaves for medicine. She was growing old, and didn't always have the strength to go to the farm, but she made sure that she kept herself busy with tasks that she could do.

'We've missed your singing, Amma. Isn't the Lord Jesus your friend any more? Come, tell me! What is the matter?' Then Amma poured out her heart to her, telling her of her frustration in not being able to read her Bible.

'So, what has happened? Doesn't God answer prayer any more?' she asked, 'or, tell me, is it that you have forgotten to ask him?'

Amma hung her head. Then together they bowed their heads to pray.

'Now then,' encouraged the old woman, 'we believe that God has heard us, and that he is going to answer, don't we?' Amma nodded. 'And he loves to hear you singing, you know.'

It was a different girl who ran back to take the bucket from her friend. She felt sure now that God would answer her prayer, but how? He didn't seem to be changing the grandmother. She was as unwilling as ever for Amma to run into the room for a few minutes with the precious book. She couldn't get up in the night and read for that would mean lighting a lamp, but somehow, God must help her.

* * * * *

'Ting! Ting! Ting!' they heard, one afternoon. 'It is the sewing woman,' the children called, as the familiar figure of Auntie Adwoa came up the forest trail, her sewing machine firmly balanced on her head. The bobbin bounced musically up and down as she walked, announcing her trade.

'Madame!' the grandmother called, welcoming

her into her courtyard, 'I have work for you.' She brought out some shirts that needed mending, and while she worked she sat and consulted with her in a low voice. The next time Amma passed through she called her. 'This is the one,' she told her. 'Could you make her a uniform? And the boy?' Amma stood, her mouth open. She was afraid to express the hope that was rising in her heart. But Kofi was more forward. 'Are we going to school, Grandmother? Are we really going to school?'

'It is your Grandfather,' she explained. 'He left the money for your uniforms and books before he went away. But you'll have to get up early and do your chores before you go,' she warned.

'Oh, I will, Grandmother, I will! Oh, thank you, thank you.' She wanted to run off straight away and tell Maame Akwia, but she had to wait for an opportunity.

'I'll be able to take my Bible to school and read it there,' she confided.

'Maybe not the first day. You get to know the teacher and then ask him first,' she cautioned.

'Of course you may bring it,' was Mr. Boateng's reply. He was pleased with his diligent pupil, and was happy to allow her to stay in to read when the others went out to play. Sometimes he would give her a passage to prepare, and ask her to read it to the class.

'Oh, Maame Akwia, thank you for praying.' Amma shared each answered prayer with her. 'But, she added, 'it is a difficult book to understand.'

'Well, we'll pray about this too,' she assured her. 'Cannot God also help you in this?'

'Amma,' Mr.Boateng called a few days later, when once more Amma was alone in the class. 'I have a little book here that may help you in your Bible reading. It is called "Light on your Path." It tells you where to read and then tells you a little about it.

'Oh, thank you, sir, thank you,' cried Amma. How wonderfully God was answering her prayers, but when a few days after this, she saw Mr.Owusu come to the school, she began to wonder what had gone wrong.

Kwame Owusu had been born in the village, but he had long since left and had become a very successful business man. Amma had heard the children calling out as he had driven as far as the bridge in a taxi. They had run out to watch him as he had walked up in his fine city suit, one of the older girls proudly carrying his suitcase on her head.

'He comes to visit his father,' she was told. 'But he doesn't come very often. He travels overseas on business.'

She had seen him arrive the previous weekend, but now, why should he come to the school? There were no children in his family.

'Get out your work books,' the teacher commanded, as he stepped out onto the verandah to talk to the visitor. The children all dutifully opened them, but their eyes were not on the pages. They saw the two men deep in conversation, and then the teacher turned and they could see his eyes sweeping the class.

'He's talking about you, Amma,' one of them whispered, when he had turned back to his visitor. Amma had her eyes cast down, for she had already been conscious of the searching looks. What could it mean? Was there some trouble? But how could Mr. Owusu have anything to do with her? Oh, surely, now that God had so wonderfully made a way for her to come to school and have opportunity to read her Bible, it wasn't to be taken from her?

'Amma, would you come here a moment please,' the teacher called. 'And the rest of you get on with your work.'

Amma left her seat and stepped onto the verandah, trembling. What could it mean? Oh, what could it mean?

Chapter 8
SUNDAY SCHOOL

'Amma! Why haven't you changed out of your school uniform? Doesn't the grandmother need you to help with the meal?'

Amma laughed. 'Oh, Maame Akwia, that is what I have come to tell you. It is so wonderful. Oh, how the Lord Jesus is answering our prayers. I will never forget to ask him again.'

'Well, what has happened?' The old lady could see that the girl was almost too excited to tell her. 'Come now, calm down and let me hear all about it.'

Amma pulled up a stool and sat down beside her friend.

'You know we prayed that I would have time to read my Bible, and then the grandfather left money so that I could go to school.'

'Yes, yes, of course I know all that.' She wanted her to get on for she could see that there was more to come.

'Well, last Friday, Mr.Owusu visited our school. He came to ask the teacher if there was someone who would go and read the Bible to Agya Asiaman and so Mr. Boateng asked me if I would like to.'

'But what about your grandmother? It was wonderful that she even allowed you to go to school, for you are such a good worker.' Once again Maame Akwia interrupted.

'Yes, I said that, but Mr.Owusu said that Papa Asiaman would pay her, and so now she is quite happy, and I go there every day, as soon as I finish school. Then I wash the pots for Grandmother after the meal.'

'I heard that Mr.Owusu had helped Agya Asiaman to become a Christian. Poor old man, with this sickness that has affected his eyes, and all the trouble his son causes he surely needs someone to help him. I'm glad he is trusting in Jesus. He has no one else to read to him, for his older son has travelled, and his daughters did not go to school; and that good for nothing Kwabena certainly wouldn't. So, why aren't you there now, Amma?'

'Oh, he isn't quite ready. So I took the chance to come and tell you.'

'I'm glad, my dear, very, very glad. Truly, God is answering our prayers above all we could have hoped for.'

'Amma!' Kofi called, 'Papa is ready now.'

'I ask permission to leave, Maame.' She bobbed respectfully, and ran off, her Bible wrapped in a cloth and carried gracefully on her head. When she entered the courtyard there was the blind man, seated in an arm chair on his verandah. A stool had been placed ready for Amma, but it was not only the faithful Kofi, but some of his friends too, who were gathered around.

'Hello, what is this?' asked Amma. 'Sunday School?'

'Papa said we could,' asserted Kofi. 'We want to hear the story too.'

'Well, in that case I think that you should sing for Papa, and then we'll pray, like we do when the pastor comes.'

And so the children sang the joyful songs that they had learned, and they clapped and danced. Other children joined them so that when it was time for the Bible reading Amma had quite a congregation.

'I am the Good Shepherd,' Amma began, but this was not so interesting for the children, and as she read on they began to fidget, and some to drift away. Kofi, who basked in his sister's glory when she was honoured, was not happy about this.

'Amma,' he interrupted, 'why don't you tell us a story like you do to me before I go to sleep. The Bible is hard for us to understand.'

'Very well,' she replied. 'I'll tell you the story first, and then I'll read it out of the Bible, and you must listen hard to see if I told it properly. Is that alright, Papa?'

Agya Asiaman was quite happy. He had been finding it hard to understand himself. And so began Amma's story hour. Her school teacher, or sometimes the pastor, would advise which stories were suitable, and find them for her in the Bible. Then she would read and practice them in her free time at school.

Once Amma had seen Agya Asiaman's son appear at the gate of the compound as the children were singing. He had made a rude gesture, and she was thankful that he had not come in to disturb them. He had stopped her, however, as she'd made her way home.

'A school girl, are we now?' he'd sneered. 'Aren't we going up in the world. To think my father has to resort to a poor little village girl like you to read to him.'

'If you were the son that you should be, there would be no need for me to go and read to him,' she had wanted to retort, but she had bitten her tongue. She had seen he had been drinking again, and knew that it was best to get out of his way as quickly and quietly as possible.

One day, there was a message waiting for Amma when she got home from school. The blind man did not want her to come that day. Sadly she changed out of her uniform and applied herself to the household tasks. She had been so encouraged by her growing 'Sunday School', as every one called it. The pastor had come along with a roll of pictures to help her in her task. She asked the children to describe what they could see to the blind man, for in that way everyone was learning. Then, one day, her teacher had come to visit them and had brought her a small blackboard and chalk. The children were proud to read the texts so that the old man could learn with them. But if he didn't want her to come then all this would come to an end, There was no way that the grandmother would allow her the free time if she wasn't receiving her wages, and the fact that they met with Agya Asiaman gave authority to what she was doing.

What could be wrong, she asked herself? Was he ill? Or did he no longer love to hear the words of life that they found in the Bible?

The next day she went straight to Agya Asiaman's courtyard. At least she would be able to see him, even if he did not want her to read. The courtyard seemed empty. There was no papa, sitting waiting in his chair; no children gathered around with their little stools, already singing praising songs in expectation of her coming.

'Agoo,' Amma called as she stood hesitating in the gateway, unsure of getting an answer. 'May I come in?'

A woman came out of one of the rooms. She put a finger to her lips, and beckoned Amma.

'Papa is in his room,' she whispered. 'He is sick.'

'Can't you take him to the doctor?' Amma was concerned. 'The doctor wouldn't be able to help him.' 'Is it?' Amma hesitated, afraid to put her fears into words. 'Is it his son? Has he been troubling him?'

The woman nodded her head. 'Oh, that boy, he is a bad one. He will be the death of his father.'

Just then the door moved and Amma heard Agya Asiaman's voice. 'Is that you, Amma?' he called. 'Come! Come and talk with me.'

Amma was awestruck to be invited into his room. She sat on the edge of a chair but kept her eyes from looking around at the treasures that he might have gathered.

'How are you?' the old man asked, 'And how is all your household?'

'They are all fine,' she assured him for they had to go through the formal greetings.

'And you, Papa? How are you? Is there any trouble?'

'I am fine,' he answered her. 'We are all fine. There isn't any trouble,' but she could see from his downcast look that there was.

'Papa,' she ventured, after an uneasy silence. 'God's book would help you if you are sad. Wouldn't you like me to read to you?'

'Ah,' he sighed. 'How can I be a Christian? What is the use of me learning about the Bible, when I have a son who is such a disgrace to me.' He sat, with his head bowed. 'You have heard?'

'No, Papa, I haven't heard anything, but I have met your son, and I know that he is a trouble to you.'

'He has taken all my money. Always the police are coming to demand money because of his crimes, and now he himself has started begging me for it. I know it is only used to buy drink and drugs.'

'Yesterday my son came and demanded money. I have no more to give him. In any case, Mr.Owusu has told me that I should not give money to help him in his bad ways. When I refused to give him anything he became very angry. I could hear from the way he was breathing that he was furious. Just then my daughter came in, and she screamed. She called for the others to come quickly, and he ran away.'

The old man put his head in his hands, and began to sob. 'He was going to kill me,' he blurted out, between his crying.

The young woman came in and, signalling for Amma to leave, sought to comfort him.

Amma found Kofi and some of the children gathered by the gate.

'Aren't we going to have Sunday School?' they asked her. Amma shook her head.

'Papa is very sad,' she told them. 'We must pray for him.'

'Shall we pray now, Amma?' It was Kwaku who made the suggestion.

'Why, yes, Kwaku. Why not? Come, let us crouch down here together, and we will all pray.'

There was a murmur, as the children each prayed quietly and earnestly for the blind man, and for his wayward son too. As their prayers came to an end, Amma heard Kofi pray, 'And Lord, please make him want to hear the Bible again, because we do want to have Sunday School.'

'God answers prayer in the morning,' she started to sing and the children joined in,

'God answers prayer at noon.' They finished the chorus together, and then someone else started up,

'Jesus hears and answers prayer.'

Amma stood up. 'I had better get back to help Grandmother,' she announced, but just then the young woman came and laid her hand on the girl's shoulder.

'Papa says, come and read to him. Perhaps you can cheer him up.'

How the children sang and danced, for even the smallest of them knew that God had answered one prayer; and with the faith of little children they felt that there was nothing he could not do.

But Amma was searching her heart. How could she find a passage that could meet the need of this heart-broken old man? She knew so little of the Bible herself. In the end she decided that she had better turn to the passage in 'Light for our Path.'

'What do you think?' she read, 'If a man owns a hundred sheep, and one of them wanders away, will he not leave the ninety nine on the hills and go to look for the one that wandered off?'

'That's my boy,' Papa sighed, his sightless eyes alight, as she finished reading. 'He is like that sheep. He has wandered off. Oh, if only the Good Shepherd would find him.'

'We are going to pray, Papa. We are all going to pray, aren't we, children? We are going to pray every day, that Jesus will bring him back and that he will be a good son to you.' And so they did. Every day as they gathered, they would pray for Kwabena.

Kwabena did not come back to torment his father again, not after the terrible day when he had raised a knife to attack him, but from time to time there was news of him. It was never good news, and it did not seem that God was answering their prayers. Though his father's heart was breaking, still the children prayed and asked the Lord Jesus to change Kwabena.

Then one day Amma looked out of the open window of her classroom and saw the blind man's daughter come hurrying up the path.

'Excuse me,' she blurted out to the teacher, 'but my father has had terrible news, and he is crying out for Amma to come to him. Please sir, will you give permission for her to come?'

Amma's heart sank as she rose in response to Mr. Boateng's signal. What could it be? She felt in her heart that it had something to do with Kwabena. Then what had happened to all their prayers? Hadn't God heard them? Or could it be that even so great a God was unable to answer?

Chapter 9
KOFI TO THE RESCUE

'So tell me, Amma! With all that weeping and wailing in Agya Asiaman's courtyard, I had thought that Kwabena was dead.'

'No, he isn't dead; though sometimes I almost wish that he were.' Amma spoke bitterly, glad that Nana Kwia was not able to look into her face, for the older girl was plaiting her hair.

It was a luxury for Amma to be able to sit quietly in pleasant company, for it could take a couple of hours for her friend to take her wiry curls and turn them into an intricate pattern of plaits. Her mother used to do it for her occasionally, as a great treat. When Nana Kwia took advantage of the fact that the grandmother was away for a couple of days and offered to do it, Amma was thrilled. Now was a chance for the girls to have a quiet conversation.

'Why ever do you say that, Amma? I know he was always horrible to you, but that is a terrible thing to say, and especially for a Christian.'

'Oh, I know, Nana Kwia. I am sorry. It isn't that I hate him. I do want him to get better and I pray every day.'

'Well, why then? Tell me.'

'Why, you see, because Kwabena is in hospital, his father has gone to stay with a relative who lives nearby. Then he can go and see him every day. That means no more Bible reading.'

'You enjoyed that, didn't you?'

'Oh, yes, I did; and you see we were having Sunday School at the same time. Most of the children in the village used to come. Now, because of Kwabena having that accident, it has finished.'

'They were on the railway line, I heard.'

'Yes. Oh, that track. I hated it the first time I ever went on it. I had a terrible fear come over me.'

'Hey! Come on! How can I plait your hair if you don't sit still?' the girl complained, for Amma had suddenly leaned forward and put her head in her hands.

'Sorry.' Sitting upright, she told her of the journey into the central market with her mother, of the mangled minibus they had seen, and the story they had heard of the driver running for his life.'

'But everyone goes that way. It is a short cut.' Some of the other women had come to join the hair dressing party. 'Everyone knows when a train is due anyway, and it makes such a noise. You can hear it from miles away. I never heard of anyone getting knocked by a train.'

'But they had been drinking, hadn't they?'

'That's right. They were probably showing off and daring each other who would stay on the track the longest.'

'Who was it who was killed?'

'Kwadwo. His father is a very rich man, from the city. He was his first born son. No money will make up for that.'

'And what about Kwabena?' another asked.

'No, he isn't dead,' Amma told them, 'but he is very, very ill. He is in a coma, and the doctors say they don't know if he will ever come out of it. But we are praying for him,' she added, 'and we know that God answers prayer.'

Yes, I do know that God answers prayer, she thought. She knew it was an answer to prayer when she was first asked to read the Bible to Kwabena's father. But what had happened now? Had God forsaken them? Didn't he love them anymore? And what about Mother? She and Kofi prayed every day, but there was not even a word or message from her; it was as if they had been abandoned for good.

'Kofi!' Amma called one morning as she was sweeping the house, her voice sharp with vexation.

'What is it Amma?' he asked, running obediently in answer to her call.

'Look! Our swallows nest. It has fallen down and is all broken to bits.' It had been one of her pleasures to watch the little birds swooping into the verandah, painstakingly building a little house of mud in which to lay their eggs.

'Did Osei Yaw do it? Oh! I feel so angry.' Nana Kwia came up behind her and quietly put a calming hand on her shoulder. She understood the frustration of the girl. Amma had had so many disappointments that this small thing, must seem to her like the last straw.

'Don't be angry, Amma,' she consoled. 'I don't suppose the children did it. These swallows nests are very fragile. They often fall down. But look here. Haven't you noticed? They have already started to build again.'

So they had. Amma was amazed. Such a terrible disappointment for the little creatures. All those days of work gone to nothing, but of course they didn't have time to sit and weep. There were eggs to be laid. They just had to get up and start again.

'Maame Akwia,' Amma confided, the next time she had an opportunity to visit the old lady, 'those swallows really taught me a lesson. I had been feeling so disappointed. There is no more Bible reading - although of course my teacher still lets me read at school, and no more Sunday School with the children. But those little birds didn't give up, and I mustn't give up either. Only I really don't know how to begin again.'

'Why, Amma. I am so glad you have come to me. I needed the message of the swallows too, for I have been feeling discouraged as well. You see, the pastor hardly ever comes to our village now to teach us. He told us that we should hold a service on a Sunday, even if he is not able to come. But you know how it is. The men are all good Christians if the minister is here, but if they know he is not coming they all arrange to be away, in case they are asked to take the lead. At first everyone was keen to help to build a church, but now no one is bothering. Look what has happened. We all worked hard to make the bricks, and the walls are nearly up, but if there is no roof on before the rains come, they will all be washed away. All our hard work will have been for nothing.'

The two bowed their heads. 'Oh Lord, please show us what to do. We do want to be like the swallows, not giving up but working hard for you, but please show us how. Amen.'

'Have you got a lesson ready for Sunday School?' Maame Akwia asked, almost as soon as they had finished praying. It was as though she had heard God speak, and now she knew what to do.

'Why, yes.' Amma looked surprised. 'I was telling the story of Joseph, before Kwabena had his accident.'

'Ask your teacher to help you prepare, and we'll have Sunday School in the church on Sunday. Never mind if the men won't come. We'll call all the women, and the children. We can sing and pray, and you can take Sunday School and read to us all from the Bible.'

And so it was that Sunday by Sunday a band of faithful women met in the shell of the little church. They had to carry their own stools with them, and they watched the weather, knowing that they needed the rain to germinate the seeds they had sown in their farms, and yet fearing for the mud baked walls.

Amma, unwanted, a slave in Maame Appiah's household, became their teacher, and instructed them in the word of God.

'The children aren't coming to Sunday School today,' Kofi declared one Sunday morning.

Amma felt her heart lurch, and then slide down to the pit of her stomach. 'Why do you say that Kofi?' she demanded, crossly. She had worked so hard to prepare her lesson.

'Don't you know?' he answered. 'The fetish priest in the next village is going to sacrifice a goat. He will dance, and then there will be a feast. Everyone is going.'

'Not everyone,' Amma replied. 'Those who love Jesus will come to church and listen to his word. This is God's day. You know that Kofi. When they had the market in the town on a Sunday, Maame Akwia and some of the women who really love Jesus wouldn't go. They lost some trade, but God was pleased with them. Well, I'm going to church, even if no one else comes. Aren't you coming with me?' But Kofi had run off.

So, her chores finished, Amma washed herself and put on her best cloth. She picked up her Bible and her stool, and made her way to the unfinished building. It was she who took the piece of iron and struck it on the bar hanging ready from a tree, thus sounding out the call to church. She sat inside, her head bowed. It was hard to find the words to say, for her heart was heavy. Had she come to spend an hour alone? But no, she should have known. Maame Akwia and some of the other faithful women soon joined her. Well, at least they could have a prayer meeting, and sing praising songs to their Saviour.

'Where are the children?' Maame Akwia whispered?'

'Haven't you heard? The priest in the next village is going to dance.'

'Yes, I know that. But have they all gone? Even your Kofi?'

Amma hung her head. She didn't want the old lady to see the tears that she couldn't keep back. That her faithful Kofi, her shadow, should have left her to go with the children to a pagan festival. She could not believe it, and yet - it must be so, for where was he?

'Come, sisters, we will pray,' exhorted one of the women. 'We know that God is the same. The pastor may not be here, but God is here, and he will listen to our prayers.'

'Oh, Lord Jesus, we are here because we love you,' Amma prayed. She knew she should pray that God would keep the children from the evil powers of the fetish priest and bring them again to his house; but somehow, she felt too heartbroken. When she had been teaching the children they had been so responsive. She had really believed that they loved God and his word, and that they were praying from their hearts; but now, where were they? Once again she thought of the little swallows, and how they must have felt when they found their nest lying smashed on the ground, but how could she have their courage to get up and carry on?

The murmur of the women's prayers was dying down.

'Who has a praising song,' asked Maame Akwia, but there was no need for anyone to strike one up. From far away they could hear a little children's song, a song of praise to Jesus, and it was coming nearer.

'The children,' they exclaimed. 'The children are coming! Oh, hallelujah! Thank you, Lord Jesus, thank you.'

'What happened, Kofi? What made them change their minds?' Amma whispered to her little brother, after they had all danced their way in and settled down. He had come and squeezed beside her on her stool.

'I went and told them what you said,' he answered. 'that if we loved Jesus we would come to Sunday School. I met some on them on the road and I told them.'

'Oh, how I love Jesus,' Amma began to sing.

'Oh, how I love Jesus,' responded the women.

'Oh, how I love Jesus,' joined in the children. They all united in song. They sang and sang. The women took off their cover cloths and swept them out in worship as they danced. The little children were clapping and leaping.

But gradually the singing died down and a hush came over the congregation, as they became conscious that some men were standing outside the little church, watching them. How long they had been standing there? No one knew. Who were they, and what could they want?

Chapter 10
NEWS OF MOTHER

'Amma! Amma!' Kofi called, rushing into the courtyard where Amma was busy coaxing the fire under the cooking pot. She looked up, her eyes watering from the smoke.

'What is it, Kofi?' She was tired, but her weariness soon disappeared when he shared the exciting news.

'Why, a lorry, Amma. The men are all down by the bridge making it strong so that it can come over.'

'What is it then? What is on it?' The women were gathering round now to hear the news.

Kofi was enjoying his role as bearer of good tidings, for the other children could not drag themselves away from the scene of all the activity.

'Why, it's the iron for the church roof,' he told them. 'There are some men who have come to fix it for us.'

Amma leaped up, clapping her hands with joy. She was about to grab her brother's hand and rush off with him when she remembered her duties. Sadly she turned back to the fire. 'You go, Kofi. I'll come as soon as I can.' She went to seat herself, but felt someone gently push her off the stool. Maame Appiah lowered herself onto it, taking her place.

'I'll see to this, girl,' she told her gently. 'You deserve to go and see. If it wasn't for you, yes, and your little brother, we wouldn't have a church in our village. And now to think that we are going to have one with an iron roof, and our own pastor to teach us too.'

'Oh! Maame!' Amma, overwhelmed by this unexpected kindness, used the name as a term of endearment. Briefly she stooped to caress her grandmother's broad shoulder before she slipped away.

'Does grandmother like us now?' asked Kofi, as they ran along to the scene of all the excitement. The lorry was over the bridge by now, and lumbering up through the village. The walls of the church had been repaired and, after helping to unload, the children sat and chatted as the carpenters fastened the rafters into place.

'She always loved us really, Kofi,' his sister explained, 'but she was cross because she had too many children to look after and there was always so much work to do. But you are right, she is certainly different these days.'

'But...' Amma looked at her brother when he didn't go on, and saw that his little lip was trembling and a tear was tumbling from his eye.

'What is it?' she asked, putting her arm around him.

'We've still got our own mother, haven't we?' he

blurted out, after a lot of sniffing and snuffling.

'Yes, of course we have, Kofi. And she is coming back to get us. We ask Jesus every day, don't we?'

There was a diversion as Amma scrambled to fetch a tin of nails for one of the workmen. The villagers were all gathering round, full of pride that they should have such a fine church to grace their village.

'And it is all through you, Kofi,' Amma whispered. 'If you hadn't gone and fetched the children that Sunday morning, then the men that Mr. Owusu sent would have gone away again and told him that we didn't deserve a church.'

'Is that what happened?' It was Nana Kwia who had joined them.

'Yes. Mr. Owusu wanted to help us build a church, but he wasn't going to spend his money unless he knew that we were serious about having one. He knew that the people would have filled the church if he came himself, so he sent his friends instead.

'He has paid for this work to be done?'

'Yes, and he has arranged for a young man to be our pastor. Agya Asiaman is giving him a room in his house, and all the people have to help with his food. Pastor Kwesi will come sometimes to see that he is getting on alright.'

'Are you sad, Amma?'

'Sad?'' Amma was startled by her friend's question. 'Why should I be sad?'

'Well, if he is living with Agya Asiaman, he will read the Bible to him. He won't need you anymore.

And he'll teach the children too I expect.'

'I suppose I am a little sad,' she admitted. 'I did love telling the stories to the children. But we'll have church nearly every night with our own pastor, and we'll be able to learn much more about the Bible.'

'But, Amma!' Kofi was tugging at her arm, trying to get a word in. 'I heard Pastor Kwesi talking to Maame Akwia, and he said that the new pastor would be glad if you would help him with the Sunday School, and that she should look round for some other young people so that he could train them, and she said, "What about Nana Kwia?".

'For shame, Kofi. You shouldn't have been listening,' she scolded, but nevertheless she turned to her friend with glee. 'Oh, Nana Kwia, would you? It would be fun to do it together.' Just then they saw Mr. Owusu himself walking toward them. He wasn't in his usual city clothes, but was looking very imposing in a Ghanaian cloth. A young man who accompanied him was in a white shirt and grey trousers.

'Here are some of your most faithful members,' he told him. 'And this young man,' he said, chucking Kofi under the chin, 'our greatest evangelist.'

'This is your new pastor,' Mr. Owusu told them, after exchanging formal greetings.

'Is Agya Asiaman home?' someone asked, on hearing that their new pastor, Jonas, was staying at his house.

'We brought him back with us,' he answered.

'Is Kwabena better then?' Amma didn't like to

interrupt the adults, but she whispered her question to one of the women, who passed it on.

'He isn't better, but he is showing just the slightest signs of response. Some pastors from the city came with us to pray for him, and although he doesn't open his eyes, the nurses are sure that there is some recognition. Pastor Jonas is going to go with Agya Asiaman to visit him, and he will read the Bible and pray with him.'

'Oh, praise God, praise God,' Maame Akwia exclaimed. 'We stayed up for a whole night to pray for him, and I know that God heard us.'

'Amma!' It was Osei Yaw. Amma didn't wait to hear what the summons was. She realised that she had been away far too long. Breathlessly she ran back to the compound and took over her duties. She was only thankful that Grandmother didn't shout angrily at her. The lady was certainly changed these days.

The new church was soon completed, and their young pastor faithful in preaching the word. He visited every home, and the people supported his services. Each evening Maame Appiah would make sure that the meal was over and the dishes washed in time for them all to go to God's house.

'Well, well. We have a happy family now,' remarked Grandfather, the next time he came home. He couldn't help but notice the difference in the atmosphere. 'And how you children are growing. Kofi a school boy now, and as for you, Amma. Your mother won't know her little girl. She'll come home to find a young lady.'

'Oh, grandfather,' Amma asked, made bold by this compliment. 'I suppose you haven't heard any news of Mother, have you?'

Grandfather rubbed his beard before he spoke, and Amma waited expectantly. 'Well, as a matter of fact..' he began.

'Yes?' Amma wanted to drag the news out of him.

'I met a friend who heard that she was trading in a town up north.'

'She is back in Ghana then? What is the name of the town?' she asked, overcome with joy that at last there was news of her. 'Is it far? Do you go there, Grandfather? Could you take us there? Oh, Kofi! Kofi!' she shouted, running off to share the news before she burst. She soon came back to ask him again. 'Could you, Grandfather? Could you?'

'Even if I was going there, you could never stand all the rattle and shaking of a long lorry ride. In any case, you might not find her when you got there, and then what would I do with you?'

'Oh, I know we would. I know we would,' she affirmed. 'Jesus would help us.'

'Couldn't we go on our own, Amma?' Kofi asked the next morning after they had prayed together.

'Yes, we could. We will.' Amma was definite. 'I'll make baskets again, and we'll go into the city and get a ride from the lorry park.'

'Not on the railway line?' Kofi was hesitant, remembering their last journey to the central market.

'No, silly. You go and gather some rushes while I do my work, and then after school I'll start to make a basket.'

But somehow the baskets didn't go right. Maame Appiah wasn't so cooperative this time, though whether she had guessed why the children wanted the money, they didn't know.

'Oh, Maame Akwia, please pray. Pray that we will get the money quickly and that we will be able to go and find mother.' But Maame Akwia was silent, and Amma went on her way feeling cross and disgruntled.

She felt disappointed with the old lady, and began to take another way when she went to the well, rather than meet her. But then she found that it was not just Maame Akwia that she was avoiding. As she was tidying her room she realised that, though she had still been going to church, it was a few days since she had had her own quiet time of Bible reading and prayer. She knew it was time to put things right. It was no use avoiding Maame Akwia, for maybe in avoiding her she had been avoiding the Lord Jesus too. She had better go and have a talk with her.

'If there was no food up north, and I knew that in going there you would die of hunger, do you think I would ask Jesus to help you?' Maame Akwia asked.

'But Maame, of course there is food. Otherwise my mother would not stay there.'

'There is more than one kind of food, Amma,' the old woman explained. 'Since Pastor Kwesi came for the campaign and especially now when we have our own pastor, we are having food for our spirits, and we are all becoming strong Christians. But if you went somewhere where there was no church, and not many of the people were Christians, do you think you would still be strong? You might even forget about the Lord, and reading the Bible, and die in your spirit.'

'Oh, Maame, I would never do that. I read my Bible every day.'

'Well, my dear, you pray about it. And I'll pray about it too. I know you want to see your mother, but don't forget we love you too.'

As Amma called to Kofi and they ran off together to school she felt a little unease in her heart. 'I would never forget to read my Bible,' she had told Maame Akwia, and yet she knew that even here, in this place, with church almost every night, she had been forgetting. And only that morning Nana Kwia had told her that they had missed her singing. She tried to sing now, but somehow there was no joy in the melody.

'Oh, How I love Jesus.' Did she really love him, or was she so full of what she wanted that she had forgotten him? There was a heaviness in her heart all day.

That night, after the pastor had told them a story, he brought out a bundle of sticks. 'Now,' he said, 'I want to show you something. Which of you is very strong?'

Of course, it was Osei Yaw who was out before anyone else.

'Are you strong enough to break this stick?' Snap!

In a moment it was done. 'That's nothing!' boasted the boy.

'Ah, but now wait a moment. Here is another stick, just the same as that one, but this time you won't be able to break it.'

'Oh yes I will,' again he boasted.

'I don't think so,' laughed the pastor, and taking the stick he tied it into a bundle of other sticks. 'Now try.'

Osei Yaw tried and tried. In the end he had to give up. Then the pastor explained. This stick is only weak and thin. On its own, anyone can break it, but when it is together with others, no one can break it.

'This is a parable,' he told them. 'None of us are strong on our own. That is why God has given us a church. Only when we are together are we strong. Don't ever think that you are strong enough to be a Christian on your own, because we have an enemy, Satan. If we stay together and pray together he can never overcome us, but if we are on our own he can easily do it.'

Amma walked home quietly. She knew that the message was for her. She had thought that even if there were not other Christians when she went to be with her mother she would still be alright. But she did so want to go and find her. Grandmother was much kinder now, and yes, she loved the little church and teaching Sunday School, but she did so want to go and be with her mother, and she had nearly enough money saved up for the lorry fare. What should she do?

Chapter 11
KWABENA MAKES A DECISION

'Oh, Nana Kwia, ' Amma sighed, as the girls paused in their task of washing their clothes. 'If only I could train to be a seamstress like you. Kwabena was right. All I'll ever be good for is to cook and farm and go to market, - and look after other people's babies,' she added bitterly. She turned her head away so that the older girl might not see her tears. But her friend understood.

'Oh, Amma, you should really go to secondary school. The teacher told Grandfather that you were his best pupil. I heard him telling Grandmother, but he said he couldn't afford to send you. She said it was no use your training to be a seamstress because they never know if your mother will return and take you away.

'Oh, Amma -' she turned and gave her a little hug, for she was looking so dejected. 'I know you wanted to go up north to look for your mother, but I'm glad that you decided to stay. I would miss you terribly. We all would.'

Amma stood up and once again bowed herself to

her task, rubbing and scrubbing as if she were taking vengeance on her garments. 'I know I did what was right,' she said after a long pause. 'After all, Kofi and I have always prayed, "Please bring Mother back to us." Suppose God had answered that prayer and Mother came back here and we had gone up north! But it is such a long time, and sometimes I wonder if I would recognise her if she did come. I try to remember what she looks like, but it is like a picture that is faded out. Maybe we should just forget about her and get on with life here. I'll just be a villager, as Kwabena said.'

'Oh, that boy!' Nana Kwia was angry. 'He is just a horrible boy! But who knows? We have all been praying for him so much, and they say he is getting better. Perhaps he will be different when he comes out.'

Amma laughed. 'He did have a bang on the head. Yes, who knows. It may have knocked all the badness out and some goodness in.'

Nana Kwia was glad to see her throwing off the gloom. As they walked up the path, their heavy baskets balanced proudly on their heads, they saw Kofi running to meet them.

'Agya Asiaman wants you to come and read to him, Amma,' he informed her, proud to be the bearer of good tidings, for he knew that his sister had missed her visits to the blind man.

'Why, I thought the pastor would be reading to him,' she answered, but Kofi knew from the hug that she gave him that she was none the less delighted. 'Tell him that I will come as soon as I have finished these jobs.'

'No, you wash yourself and go, girl. Let some of the others do the work for a change.' Grandmother spoke roughly, but Amma felt overwhelmed by her kindness. She ran happily across the village, Kofi skipping proudly behind.

'Agoo - May I come in?' she called as she came to the courtyard.

'Amee - come.' Agya Asiaman was sitting in his old rocking chair on his verandah, and some of the children had already pulled up their stools in expectation of Amma's visit.

'So you have forgotten your friend,' he rebuked her gently.

'Oh, Papa! No! But you have the pastor to read to you now,' she began.

'He has gone into the hospital to visit Kwabena for me,' he told her. 'I am an old man. I can't travel to and fro. Now that I know that my son is on the mend I can rest here while Jonas goes for me. Besides, he can teach him how to walk in God's way much better than I can. But you have been as a daughter to me, Amma. You must not forget to visit an old man. We have missed her, haven't we?' he asked, turning to the children, whose number had swelled by now. 'Come now, what about a song for Amma?'

And so they sang, and then they prayed for their young pastor, that God would use him to lead Kwabena to walk in God's way. 'Amen!' they all said, 'Amen!' Then the blind man added his own prayer.

'And Lord, remember your young servant, Amma, how she would love to see her mother. Please speak to this young woman's heart, so that she will remember her children, and come back to them, Amen.'

Amma had her Bible open, and was wondering what story she should turn to. It would have to be the last one they had had in church, for she had not prepared a new one, but before she could begin there was an interruption.

'Pastor, Pastor,' the children all called, running up to welcome their friend, for he always had time for them, but this time he brushed them aside.

'Oh, Father,' he called, 'please excuse me for interrupting, but I have news for you.'

'Kwabena?' The old man was on his feet, his face ashen and his hands trembling as he felt his way towards the voice but the young man grasped his hand and led him into his room.

Bewildered, Amma motioned to the children that they must go on their way. She and Kofi walked quietly home.

'What can it be?' they asked each other. 'Oh, I do hope it doesn't mean that Kwabena is worse again, and his father has to go back to the hospital. And just when he had asked me to come and read to him again.' Amma sighed. Life did seem to have so many disappointments. She slipped back to the compound and took her stick, ready to pound the palm nuts that they had harvested earlier.

'Leave that, girl,' called Grandmother, when she heard why they had returned so soon. 'That can wait. What about reading to me, if Agya Asiaman is too busy? There is a story the pastor told us - I want to hear it again.'

'Which one, Grandmother?'

'It is about an old woman, and her daughter in law laid her baby in her lap.'

Amma puzzled for a while. In the end it was Kofi who realised what story it was.

'You know, Amma. The girl who was black like us, and she went into the corn fields.'

'Ruth!' Amma turned the pages and began to read. When she had finished Maame Appiah touched her hand very gently.

'I've been thinking about that story.' She spoke quietly as if to herself. 'I had two children placed in my lap. I was very angry at the time because my step daughter deceived me, but now I know that those children were a gift from God;' and she opened her arms and gently pulled them to her. The next moment, as if ashamed of this unusual show of emotion, she pushed them off and sent them running about their tasks. But Amma, and her small brother, were comforted. Somehow God had shown them that they were not in that village because they had been dumped there, unwanted by their mother, but it was God himself who had sent them to be a blessing. It was no effort to sing now, however loudly their grandmother shouted. 'Yes, God is good, God is good to me.'

They did not have to be anxious about Kwabena for long, for word quickly spread around the village that the pastor had brought good news. It was with a spirit of anticipation that they gathered to church that night.

'I know that some of you have been praying for Kwabena for a long time,' the pastor began, 'not just because of his accident on the railway line, but before that, because he has been a grief to his parents. I believe that because of your prayers God has saved his life. You see, after the accident, the doctors said that there was no hope of his recovery.

'It was when Mr. Owusu began to read the Bible to Kwabena that he first showed signs of response,' said the pastor and so one or other of us began visiting every day and reading to him and singing and praying. Eventually he came out of the coma and now he is getting better all the time. The doctor has said that at last he can come home.'

'Oh, Hallelujah! We thank God! We thank God!' the people were shouting. Some of the women had arisen, ready to express their joy in the dance, but the pastor interrupted.

'That is not the end of the story. I am sure that when he comes home you will find him a very different person; God has spared his life, and now he wants to turn away from his bad ways and become a Christian.'

Agya Asiaman rose. 'I want to thank you all for

your prayers...' he began, but he could not go on for he was choked by the tears of joy that were springing up. At last they closed the service and as they went out Amma found the eldest daughter of the old man waiting for her.

'Papa says to be sure to come and visit him again,' she whispered. But once Kwabena was home from hospital it wasn't so easy.

'Come, Amma! We are going to welcome him!' the children had shouted, and she had joined in the triumphal procession as they met the car, shouting and cheering as it drove slowly into the village.

She had gone to the house with the others when they had made their official visit. They had brought gifts, to wish him 'life on his head,' thus thanking God for his recovery. But she did not feel that she wanted to meet the boy face to face. She knew that he was changed, for he was always faithful in the church services, but somehow she could not forget his unkind words to her. She was not even sure that he would approve of her visiting his father.

But the blind man would not be denied the visits of this one who had been more to him than his own family, and once again Kofi was sent with a summons.

'Oh, Papa, forgive me,' she pleaded, when he gently rebuked her. 'I thought ..' she hesitated, 'You have Kwabena now.'

'Kwabena is pleased to see you too, - aren't you, son?'

'Of course, Father,' he mumbled, but he hung his

head, as if he were embarrassed to look at the girl. But then, after a moments hesitation he looked up, as if he had at last found courage to face an unpleasant task.

'I wanted to see you,' he told her. 'I have told my father how sorry I am for all the trouble I have caused him, but I wanted to say that I am sorry to you too. I used to say horrible things to you. I beg of you to forgive me.'

'Why no.' Amma was distressed. 'You don't need to apologise to me. It was all true. I am a villager.'

'You are a villager we are proud of then,' added his father. 'I certainly am thankful that God sent you to us. But come, you two, you must be friends, for I need you both. Kwabena, why don't you tell Amma what happened to you in the hospital? Now then, you children, settle down, for this time Kwabena is going to tell a story.'

'Oh, Father, I can't...' he complained, but when Amma pleaded with him he began.

'I didn't remember anything after we were walking on the railway line,' he told them. 'I didn't know even that I was in the hospital. I felt as if I were deep deep down in a dark pit, but then one day I had a dream.'

'I was standing in a police court, and there were chains - on my legs and arms and round my neck and all over me, dragging me down so that I didn't have strength to remain standing. The judge was speaking to me. His voice was strong and terrible, like thunder. I couldn't see his face. It was too bright to look at, but as he was speaking, all the bad things I had ever done in my life seemed to pass before me; when I was a very small boy and I would shout and scream and beat my mother if I didn't get my own way; times I had played tricks on the teacher at school, and then all the very bad things I had done with my mates. I saw that time in the market when we had been robbing and tricking people, and I saw you, Amma and how I had abused you. In the brightness of his face I felt so ashamed, and all the people in the court were pointing at me and shouting, 'Guilty! Guilty! Guilty! He must die.' They came to drag me away and I tried to cry out for mercy but I could not make a sound.'

'Then suddenly there was a great quiet, and the light from the judge's face seemed to fill all the court, and a voice cried out, 'I have been punished in his place. Let him go free.' I could not lift my eyes to see who had spoken, but then I felt the chains falling off me, and a strength coming into my body. I looked up and all the people in the court had disappeared and only the judge was there. But he didn't look like a judge now, and I knew that it was Jesus.

'I opened my eyes and Mr.Owusu was there, reading from the Bible. After that I slept, but whenever I woke there seemed to be someone sitting there, reading or praying and all the time I could feel myself getting stronger.'

Amma was crying. 'Oh, thank you. Thank you for telling us. Oh, God is so good.' She felt as if her heart would overflow with happiness, but her tears of joy were soon to become ones of sorrow, for Osei Yaw ran into the courtyard to fetch her.

'Amma! Come quick!' He called. 'Grandmother is ill.'

Chapter 12
MOTHER

'Go away, you horrible creature!' Amma picked up a stone and threw it at the vulture that sat, like some cloaked ghoul, looking down on her. The great bird squawked angrily, but all he did was hop noisily along the iron roof, knowing he was out of reach. Amma was about to search for another missile, but she was conscious of Kofi's large eyes upon her, and turned away, ashamed.

'Don't be afraid of them, Kofi. They are horrible, ugly creatures, but they help to clear up all the rubbish, so that we don't get sick.' That is what she had told him when, as a small boy, he had run away from them in fear. 'Only the hawks, Kofi. Throw stones at them, for they are thieves. They will come and steal the baby chicks.'

She was ashamed, but how could she explain to him the anger that she felt toward them, for somehow these creatures that feed on carrion seemed to embody death. They were always waiting for something to die, looking for dead flesh; as if they were in league with death itself; death who had come and stolen the grandmother so suddenly away from them.

They had prayed so hard too. Even when Madame Appiah had been taken to the hospital in the city they had met in the church and prayed all night. Amma had been so sure that God would answer their prayers. But grandmother was dead, her body lying there, cold and still in the mortuary until all the relatives could be gathered for the funeral.

'Will Mother come?' Kofi had asked.

'I am sure that she will, if she hears in time. They have sent messages to try to reach her.' It had been Amma's one hope that this tragedy would be the means of her mother's returning; but the days had gone by. So many visitors coming to bring their condolence. So much weeping, and singing of the old woman's praises. But no Mother.

The pastor had been, the Christians with him, telling the people of the change in Grandmother, and how she had come to trust in Jesus. Amma knew, better than anyone else, of the difference there had been in her life. Without any doubt she knew that they need not be sad for her, that the old lady had gone to heaven.

She gazed at the stone that was still in her hand. Why then, was there anger in her heart? And why, when everyone else was weeping, were her own eyes as dry as this stone? Before, she had so often been embarrassed because she could not keep back the tears, but now when it was expected that she should express her sorrow she seemed empty of feeling.

Just then, she felt Kofi tugging at her hand. 'Amma, come quick. They are talking about the funeral.' She ran with him to where Grandfather was sitting, a group of relatives around him.

'Tomorrow then?' she heard one repeat.

'Yes, we cannot afford to wait any longer. We have done our best to inform all the relatives.'

Stunned, Amma stumbled away, down towards the river and slumped down, her head between her hands. Kofi, ever faithful, knew better than to speak.

At last she looked up. 'I thought that Mother would have come,' was all she said. She understood now the cause of her fear and anger, but it was Kofi who put it into words.

'Who will look after us, then?'

'I don't know, Kofi.' That was it, they wouldn't belong to anyone. It would be alright while Grandfather was home, but when he was off on his long journeys they would be at the beck and call of each of the women who lived on the compound. They could be back in the same situation they were in when their mother first left them, unloved and unwanted.

'Jesus loves us, Amma,' Kofi whispered, as if he had read her thoughts.

'Yes, Kofi, Jesus loves us. He will look after us,' and she gave him a little squeeze. At least they had each other.

'Amma!' She knelt to splash water in her face before returning to her duties, but Nana Kwia was running up the path towards her. 'Amma! Go and get washed and changed. Your grandfather wants you to come and greet some of the visitors. - You too Kofi,' she added.

To serve them, that was the usual call. She had been kept busy from dawn till dusk, carrying drinks and preparing meals, but to greet them; - that was another thing. Donning a clean skirt and the white blouse she wore for church, she shyly joined the guests.

'Amma,' Grandfather called, 'this lady says that she knows you.'

'Good morning, Madam.' Amma curtsied, and lifted her eyes shyly to meet the ones that were looking so kindly down upon her.

'Amma, do you remember me?' she asked. Amma's eyes were searching hers now as memory began to awaken. An impression of the delicious smell of cooking plantain came to her, the noises of a busy market. She was back, behind the meat stalls, looking for the relative that her mother had sent her to greet.

'Aunt Mary!' Amma cried, and ran into the arms that were already opened to her. 'Oh, Aunt Mary.'

They were sitting apart now, for they had so much to tell each other. It was Kofi who proudly brought the little book that they had treasured.

'Amma told me that you would be praying for us,' he told her, having received his own welcome.

'I did pray for you. Indeed I did,' she told them. 'Your mother had told me that she was leaving, and I knew how hard it would be for you. Indeed I did pray for you.'

'We prayed every day that Mother would come back - but - but - she hasn't come.'

Aunt Mary held out her arms to the little boy as she could see the tears about to spill over.

'What?' she laughed. 'After all the wonderful things that God has done for you, do you think that God hasn't heard that prayer? Or do you think that he cannot answer? We must believe when we pray. Doesn't it say that in your Bible?'

'But -.' Amma felt she couldn't let Kofi take the blame. 'We were so sure that she would come for the funeral, but she hasn't.'

'Maybe she has gone abroad and has not received the message. Don't worry, God is able to bring her here. Come, we will pray again, together. There is still time.'

* * * * *

'Yes, she did come,' Amma told the blind man, as she was visiting him, a few days later. The pastor was away, and Agya Asiaman had sent a message for her to come and read to him.

'She looked so fine in her funeral clothes,' she told him. 'Yes, yes, she is well.'

'You didn't bring her to visit me?' he queried. 'Your aunt Mary came to greet me before she left. She is proud of you children.'

'I did ask Mother to come with me today, Papa, but she said she hadn't changed her dress.'

'Well, maybe tomorrow.'

'What is she going to do? Will she stay here in the

village and take your grandmother's place?' It was Kwabena who asked. He usually joined in these times of Bible reading. Amma knew that he was quite capable of reading to his father himself, but she was glad that he, too, appreciated her coming. A strong friendship was forming between them.

'I don't know. She hasn't spoken to us of her plans at all. I...' Her voice broke. Now that the time for weeping was over it seemed that her own fountain of tears was opening again.

'Kofi, will you go and ask Nana Kwia to light the fire and tell her that I won't be long.' Kofi looked unwilling, as if he realised that this was just an excuse to get him out of earshot, but he was an obedient child.

'I am really afraid that she is going to leave us behind again,' she whispered. 'Kofi wants to be with her all the time, but she pushes him off and tells him to come with me. She only has time for our small sister, Akusia. She is running around now. Everyone admires her. I don't want to leave this village. I have so many good friends now; but if Mother goes off and leaves us again I think that the other women will be very angry and it won't be good for us.'

'Perhaps we should pray that she will stay here,' the old man ventured, patting her hand. 'We wouldn't like to lose them, would we, Kwabena?' Kwabena only smiled.

'Mother promised you a gift of gold,' asserted Kofi, later that evening when, once again his mother had rejected his company and sent him back to his sister.

'I know, Kofi, but she has a lot of other things to think about just now, and she did bring us some new clothes. Don't worry her about it, will you? She will remember.'

She tried to sound confident. It wasn't the gift that she was worried about, so much as the fact that Mother didn't seem to be aware of what her children had suffered. Nor did she know how hard her daughter had tried to keep her promise to her.

Whenever she went to church, or to visit the blind man, she would ask her mother to join her, but each time there was an excuse. Then one day, Amma returned from the farm to find her mother already washed and changed into one of her good dresses.

'Come, get ready,' she told her, 'before I change my mind. I am coming with you to visit the old man.'

'O Mama! Mama!' Kofi was jubilant, clinging to her skirt as they walked through the village, and this time she did not reject him.

'I didn't know you knew our songs,' Amma remarked as they returned home.

'There are a lot of things about me that you don't know,' was all her mother replied, but from that time on she came with them regularly to church.

'Do you want to come with me into the city tomorrow?' her mother asked, one day. Amma was glad that she had an excuse to refuse, but a fear was gripping her heart. She could not forget that day, so long ago now, when her mother had left them beside the baskets of charcoal while she had made plans to abandon her family in search of riches. Oh, surely, surely she was not going to arrange another trip? Should she go with her? Would it make any difference?

'Oh, Maame Akwia, please pray. Ask the other women, please. Please.'

Amma made sure that she had her mother's favourite palm soup ready for her when she got home, for she knew that she would be tired after the long journey. She did not dare ask how she had got on and her mother sat in silence, hungrily devouring the food. When the call rang out for church Amma excused herself and slipped away. She was surprised when at the end of the service she found her mother sitting there too. She must have come in late. Perhaps there was hope after all. But it wasn't until Sunday morning that her heart was set at rest.

They had had their usual joyful service. They had sung and danced. They had all stood, their arms upraised, praying at the same time. Their pastor had preached from the Bible and they had brought their gifts.

'Before we close,' he asked, 'does anyone want to tell us of how God has helped them, or of answered prayer?'

'I should have spoken about how God answered our prayers and brought Mother back to us,' thought Amma, 'only somehow it hasn't really been answered as we had hoped.' She felt ashamed that she should think such a thing, but it was true. They weren't sure that they had really got their mother back. Then suddenly everything changed.

Mother had gone to stand in the front of the church. She was holding Akusia in her arms, as if to give her courage. Tears were in her eyes and a hush fell over the congregation as she struggled to find words to express what was in her heart.

'When I was a young girl, I lived in a village where there was a church. I became a Christian, but after a while we moved away, and I forgot about God. All I thought about was getting money, and gold. I thought that this was the most important thing in the world. I left my children, as you know. Madame Appiah was an old woman, and already had too many responsibilities, but I left her to care for my children so that I could travel and become rich. I resented having to come back here, because I was losing trade, but...'

The people murmured sympathetically as she struggled once again to regain her composure.

'It is my children who have shown me true riches. I used to think that to live in a village was something to be ashamed of, but it is here, in this village that my children have become Christians. I know that this is more important that making money.

'I was planning to go back north, and leave my children again, but God has shown me that I will be far richer if I stay here and have Christian teaching, and have my children with me.'

'Keep us, Lord, keep us...'

It was Maame Akwia who started up the song, and

a volume of sound filled the little church and overflowed to the houses around as they all joined in,

'Keep us Lord,

Keep us under your wings.' There was a deep amen from Amma's heart.

'Oh Papa,' exclaimed Amma, as they were talking it over together, 'God did answer our prayer didn't he? He has brought Mother back to us. Oh, I'm so glad that we don't have to go away from here. I have so many good friends. But, Papa? Where is Kwabena? Has he gone back to school?'

The blind man was silent, his head bowed. Amma ran and knelt beside him, suddenly realising that in her joy she had not been conscious of his need.

'What is it, Papa?'

'I'm worried about him, Amma. He has been seeing some of the friends he had before he became a Christian. Now he is talking about going into the city to work. I am afraid that if he mixes with them again he may slip back into his bad ways. He needs a good church and Christian friends.'

'Yes, Papa. We all do. I know that. Oh Papa! Surely, he could not return to his bad ways, not after all that God has done for him?'

Chapter 13
THE GIFT

'But why go to the city, when you know that there are so many temptations there?'

Amma had been glad of the opportunity to express her fears to Kwabena. Finding the old man asleep when she had gone round to visit him, the two had sat quietly talking on the verandah.

Amma shared with the lad the parable of the sticks, and how it had helped her to decide not to go north in search of her mother.

'I know that you are a true Christian, Kwabena,' she explained. 'No-one can doubt that. But we all need to be with other Christians to be strong.'

The boy was quiet. He knew that what she was saying was true. A battle was waging within him.

'There are Christians in the city, aren't there?' he answered at last, defiantly, but then he added, 'in any case, I'm not content to be a villager for the rest of my life.'

Amma knew that at last he was facing up to the real reason. She remembered his cruel jibes, and as if sharing her memory, he reached out his hand and touched her lightly.

'You shouldn't be staying here either, Amma. You could go a long way. Why, look how gifted you are with the children. When you are older, any of the city churches would be glad to have you as a teacher.'

'Hey! Kwabena! Psst!' Kwabena excused himself, and slipped away. The fact that the boy calling had not wanted to come into the compound and greet his father made it obvious to Amma that he was not a true friend. A heaviness weighed on her spirit as she returned home.

Her heart was aching for Kwabena. His life had been so wonderfully changed, and yet she doubted that he had the strength of character to stand up to the temptations of city life. Yet she knew too, that her pain was as much out of self pity as of concern, for a strong friendship had been forged between the two. She would miss him very much if he went away.

It wasn't that she yearned for city life. She loved the village people and their quiet, easy going ways, content with their planting and gathering, taking each day as it came; and now, especially with Mother back and settling down among them, and the little church prospering, she knew that she of all people should be content. But she wasn't. There was a deep ache in her heart. Perhaps this was just a part of growing up? When she had first come to the village she had been a child, but she would soon be a young woman. She didn't know what it was, but knew that somehow she wanted more out of life than this.

Turning aside to a large mango tree she clambered

into its spreading branches. She and Kofi had often used it as a refuge when they had wanted to be alone, but today she was glad that he was not with her. For how could he possibly understand? She didn't understand herself, but she took comfort in remembering that there was one who did. She wasn't able to put her desire into words, nor did she have to, for her saviour read her heart and when at last she clambered down again she felt comforted.

'Amma, where have you been?' Kofi was accusing. 'I went to Agya Asiaman's house, and they said that you had left. Grandfather is calling for you.'

Grandfather, Mother with him, was sitting in his inner room, and as Amma joined them she could see that this was an important occasion.

'Amma,' Grandfather began. 'Your mother and I have been talking about what work you should do. You have been a good girl, and it isn't right that you should just remain here as everybody's servant.'

Amma's heart leapt. She had been unable to express her discontent, but she had known that God understood, and now it was as though he was speaking through the old man.

'Your Mother was talking to Mr. Boateng, your teacher,' he went on. 'He was saying how gifted you are as a teacher, and what a blessing it would be for the village if you should go to high school and then train as a teacher. Maybe you could come back to teach here.'

'Your grandfather has agreed to help me with the

school fees,' Mother went on. 'Mr. Boateng will help you to prepare for the entrance exam.'

'You will be alright, Kofi,' Amma assured him, when she shared her joy with her brother. 'You are a big boy now, and Mother is here, and you have Akusia to look after. I will be home every holiday.'

'What about Christian fellowship?' Maame Akwia enquired when she shared the news. 'You have been asking me to pray for Kwabena. You have been anxious enough about him going away from the church, but now you want to go yourself.'

'There is a good Christian fellowship in the school,' Amma replied. 'The pastor has met one of the teachers there. And I'll be home every holiday. Oh, Maame, I'm sure that it is God who is opening this door. I have such a joy and a peace, it is like a river deep down in my heart. - Oh, if only I could have this peace about Kwabena's going away. Oh, Maame, couldn't we pray?'

'Why, of course. I pray every day, and I know that you do.'

'Yes, but I mean, all together. Will you ask the pastor? Couldn't we pray all night, like we did when Kwabena was so ill in hospital? It is just as serious isn't it?'

The old lady was silent for a while. At last she spoke. 'Yes, my dear. You are right. It is just as serious. And we need good people to stay in our villages. That is the problem with our country. All the young people want to go and live in the cities, and only the old ones are left at home. Yes, indeed, we will speak to the pastor.'

'Mother didn't remember about the gift of gold, did she?' Kofi asked again one day.

'Oh, Kofi, for shame. She is spending all this money to buy my uniform and send me to high school.' Amma defended her mother, but in her heart she too felt that her mother had not kept her promise. If she had apologised and said that she could not afford it she would have felt better, but it seemed the promise had been made lightly. She tried to push the thought away. Why did Kofi have to keep on asking?

But one day, when Madame Adwoa returned from a trip to the market, she called her daughter to her.

'You must have thought that I had forgotten my promise,' she began. 'You certainly have earned your gift, for they have all told me how good you have been to Kofi. I hadn't forgotten, but there is a very skilful goldsmith. He has travelled, and I have been waiting for him to return because I want you to have something special. The next time I go to market you shall come with me and you can choose what you would like him to make for you.'

Amma threw her arms around her neck in an unusual demonstration of affection. Mother hadn't forgotten. She would have her gift of gold. Somehow all the long months of hardship and heartache seemed worthwhile. It wasn't the value of the gift, though every Ghanaian girl would value such a treasure, for was not their's the land of gold. No, it was a token that her mother truly loved and appreciated her.

'He is going to make me such beautiful earrings, Maame Akwia,' Amma told the old lady, after her visit to the goldsmith, 'all beautifully intertwined, with lovely stars hanging from them.' She babbled on, for she was so excited, and she loved to share her joys as well as her sorrows with this friend. Finding no response, her words dried up. She gazed into the wrinkled old face. Suddenly she realised that she had never ever seen this dear old Christian wearing any jewellery; no, not even on the occasion of the dedication of their new church, when everyone was resplendent in their finery.

It was hard for Amma to think of her as having ever been young, but now she paused and suddenly wondered. She had once told her that, as a young bride, she had come from another tribe. What had happened? No wonder she had understood the loneliness of the two children when they had come to the village, - and they, of course, had been among their own people. And what about her husband? Had he remained faithfully with her until he died, or had he gone off to seek riches in the city, as had happened with their own father? He had married again, never to remember his first wife, and the children he had brought into the world.

'Maame Akwia,' Amma asked, drawing close and putting her small hand over the old wrinkled one, 'haven't you ever had any gold jewellery?'

'Maybe. Maybe,' she answered, a smile playing

around her lips, 'but I've had a greater gift by far; much more precious than gold.'

Amma came away, wondering what she could have meant, her enthusiasm dampened somewhat, but Nana Kwia was there on a visit when she returned to the house, and she found a willing audience to share her joy about the earrings.

'And I have news for you,' Nana Kwia told her, when at last she was permitted to speak. 'I met Kwabena in the market, and he asked me to tell you that you must have been praying very hard, and he will see you soon.'

Amma hurried to see the blind man, as soon as she had a spare moment.

'I had the same message,' was his reply. 'I know no more than you.'

It was a week later before their curiosity was satisfied.

'Kwabena is coming,' Kofi had announced. Amma had run out to give him a wave, but she had had to be very patient before she could go to the house to greet him formally. Then all she was told was that he had some news to share in the church service that evening. At last the time came, and the pastor called the lad forward.

'I am telling you the news here, in church, because I know that you have been praying for me, and it is in answer to your prayers that I am able to stand here and tell you this.'

He paused a moment and blew his nose hard, and

some of the women unashamedly wiped their eyes, remembering how God had brought this wayward sheep back to him.

'You all know how I became a Christian, but although I loved God, I didn't want to stay in the village. I wanted to become a rich city gentleman.

'I had an offer of a job in one of the government offices, but I knew that many of the people I would be working with were not Christians and would try to lead me back into my bad ways.'

'You must have been praying for me, for before I arrived there for the interview I met Pastor Kwesi.'

'"Why Kwabena," he exclaimed. "I had been thinking about you. There is a gentleman I wanted you to meet. I didn't know how to get a message to you, but here you are."

'He took me to a room of one of the students at the university. A few of us gathered and then this man Tim came.

'He talked to us about our country once being called the Gold Coast, and about cocoa, and all the things we exported for foreign trade; he talked about people who go and sit in big offices and look so important but really they are wasting their country's money, and wasting their own lives too.'

'Then he told us that God had shown him that our real riches are in the villages. We so often despise the village people, but he said that if only we would really learn to farm properly, Ghana could be one of the most prosperous nations, instead of always being in debt.'

They looked at Kwabena. There was a glow about him. Why was he telling them all this?

'The man has a farm, where he takes young men as students and trains them, not just in farming, but in discipleship too. Then they can come back and live in their own villages and help their people to live better lives.'

'I felt that God was talking to me, because I really would love to stay in the village, only I thought that it was something to be ashamed of. Now I see that I can be working for God here.'

'So are you going to go and train with him?' the pastor asked.

'Yes, I am,' Kwabena answered proudly, 'only not yet. He wants me to go back and finish my schooling first. And I know that this is right. But I wanted you all to know that God is answering your prayers for me, and that one day you will be proud of me.'

'We are proud of you now,' thought Amma as she walked home. Surely her cup of happiness was full. They would both be going different ways, she to the girls school and he to the boys, but could it not be that God was leading them together to work for him in this village that they both loved?

In a few more days she would have her gift of gold, only, she couldn't help thinking, what had Maame Akwia meant, about "something more precious than gold?"

Chapter 14
MORE PRECIOUS THAN GOLD

'And this is the little book of Scripture verses that we hope to have published, while we are working on the translation of the whole Bible.'

As Amma listened to the young man so enthusiastically sharing with them his vision of bringing God's word to one of the remote Northern tribes, she remembered another little book of Scripture verses, one that she still regarded as among her most treasured possessions. How desolate she would have been if she had never read it and through it found the God who answered prayer.

'Oh, Maame Akwia,' she shared with the old lady when she returned to the village. She was telling her about the visit of this young Bible translator to their school Christian union, 'I so wanted to help them to get the book published. You see, I was remembering about my little book, the one Aunt Mary gave me. It was through reading it that I first learned to ask Jesus to help me; and I really believe that it was in answer to our prayer that God sent the pastor to our village to teach us how to be Christians.'

'Maybe! Maybe!' mused the old lady, a smile

playing around her lips. 'But it wasn't only in answer to your prayers, you know.'

'Was it you praying too, Auntie? Tell me,' she coaxed, seeing that there was more to come.

'Yes, perhaps I will tell you,' she conceded, 'for you are not a child any longer.'

Amma drew up a stool and settled herself beside her friend.

'My husband moved here when I was still a young woman. I had been taken to church as a child and I thought I was a Christian, but now there was no church, and I wanted to please my husband, so I used to go with him to the heathen festivals. Then my child died, and he took another wife, and he forgot about me, and I was very sad, and homesick too.'

'Poor Auntie,' Amma interrupted, patting her hand.

'Not so poor,' she replied, 'for it was my sorrow that caused me to remember the Lord, and I began to pray. I knew that I could not go back to my own people, for my mother had died long since, and so I prayed that some Christians would come to live here, and that we would have a church here, in this village.

'The years went by. It seemed so hopeless, but somehow I just couldn't give up praying. So you can imagine my joy when Pastor Kwesi came and held the campaign. That is why, when he talked about building a church, I felt that there was nothing too much for me to give.' Maame Akwia put her hand to her mouth, realising that she had said more than she had intended.

Amma's eyes were shining.

'You gave your gold jewellery, didn't you?' she accused, her eyes shining. 'Oh, Auntie, I so much wanted to help these people in the north.'

She was silent for a while, a battle waging in her heart. At last she was able to express the thoughts with which she had been struggling.

'Auntie, - do you think I could give my earrings?' Her lips faltered as she spoke, and, taking one off, she held it up, as she had done so many times, to let the light display its beauty.

The old lady stretched out her wrinkled hand and, gently taking it from her, fastened it back into its place.

'No, my dear,' she answered, 'not yet any way. Your mother wouldn't wish it. And it is good that you delight in your gift of gold, for you have earned it. I am sure that you can find some other way to help them; but I am glad now that you understand, as I do, that there is something more precious than gold.'

'Oh, Auntie, I do, I do. It is the Lord Jesus, isn't it? And just think, that if Mother hadn't gone away, and if Aunt Mary had not given me that little book, I might never have found him.'

OTHER BOOKS AVAILABLE FROM CHRISTIAN FOCUS PUBLICATIONS

FIGHT FOR FREEDOM

by Eleanor Watkins

Life seems very predictable for Caradoc until Lucius is brought to his village. Suddenly, everything changes dramatically and Caradoc's actions are to spark off a chain of events which will affect his life for ever.

ISBN 185792 033 3
£2.99 160pp

THE BROKEN BOW

by Pauline Thompson

When Kisoo agrees to meet his brother for a moonlight hunting expedition, he gets into more trouble than he expected. Breaking the stranger's bow and running away, Kisoo meets up with people who tell him about a special friend who can forgive him.

ISBN 1 87167 698 3
£2.99 128pp

THE OUTSIDERS

by Margaret Smith

Donna finds herself at logger-heads with Stewart Steele. He's an incomer to the area and she thinks he's stealing from her. But Stewart is not taking the blame, and there's another side to him besides his tough image.

ISBN 1 87167 652 5
£2.99 128pp

TRUE GOLD

by Cliff Rennie

The huge olympic stadium was full of cheering spectators. Among them was Jason, anxiously scanning his programme. Gordon's race was due to start in just a few minutes. Surely nothing or no one could stop him going for gold. Then suddenly Jason gasped in horror. Gordon was in deadly danger! But what could he do?

ISBN 1 87167 690 8
£2.99 128pp